MW00680173

ALWAYS
KILL A STRANGER

Captain Jose Da Silva Mysteries
by Robert L. Fish

The Fugitive
Isle of the Snakes
The Shrunken Head
Brazilian Sleigh Ride
The Diamond Bubble
Always Kill A Stranger
The Bridge That Went Nowhere
The Xavier Affair
The Green Hell Treasure
Trouble In Paradise

ALWAYS KILL A STRANGER

A Captain Jose Da Silva Mystery

Robert L. Fish

A Foul Play Press Book

The Countryman Press, Inc.
Woodstock, Vermont
05091

Copyright © 1967, 1988 by the estate of Robert L. Fish

All rights reserved

This edition published in 1988 by Foul Play Press, an imprint
of The Countryman Press, Inc., Woodstock, Vermont 05091

ISBN 0-88150-117-4

Printed in the United States of America

This book is affectionately dedicated
to my sister-in-law

MRS. EVA COHEN

and also, in fond memory, of my late
brother-in-law

A. MARK COHEN

ALWAYS
KILL A STRANGER

One

THE SEA, which had been so deceptively peaceful and calm when the freighter *Santa Eugenia* had discharged a portion of its cargo in Salvador de Bahia and headed south along the Brazilian coast, was now beginning to perceptibly roughen. Whitecaps flecked the growing waves beneath a dismal morning sky rapidly filling with threatening black clouds; a sudden chill touched the rising wind. The increased movement brought protesting creaks from the rusty plates of the ship, which nosed deeper into the murky green depths, as if searching for the cause of this abrupt unfriendliness. In the small galley below, dishes slid haphazardly and pots clattered; dim bulbs in the forecastle angled perilously on their twisted flex, swaying erratically, throwing monstrously distorted shadows across the stacked bunks.

On the small open bridge that jutted from the wheelhouse, Captain Enrique Juvenal, master of the *Santa Eugenia*, studied the latest radio reports of the storm into which the ship was heading, and shook his head. Captain Juvenal was worried. A cautious man by nature, he knew his beloved *Santa Eugenia* was neither the newest nor the sturdiest of freighters, and he also knew his cargo was in severe imbalance as a result of their off-loading in Salvador de Bahia. And even more he knew that the sudden tropical storms that could sweep this area, while rare, were certainly no less treacherous for that.

He leaned over the flaking rail of the bridge and stared down at his young first mate, balancing himself expertly on the pitching deck below, busily directing the shifting of the meager deck-cargo in an effort to put some semblance of security into their tenuous position. Captain Juvenal scratched his heavily bearded face and sucked fiercely on his thin black cigar; smoke billowed about him, to be instantly snatched away by the increasing gale. A respectful touch on his shoulder drew his attention; it was the radioman handing him another slip. He nodded dismissal even as he scanned the paper, frowned blackly at the message it contained, and then bent over the rail, his white teeth gleaming about the cigar.

"Miguel!"

The first mate looked up, gave one final suggestion over his shoulder to his men to prevent them from disappearing for coffee while he was gone, and trotted up the narrow companionway. He paused a moment at the top to study the darkening horizon, and then touched his cap.

"Sir?"

"How's the work going?"

The mate raised his shoulders. "Slow." His tone seemed to indicate that in his opinion it was also largely useless.

He met the captain's eye squarely. "It isn't the deck-cargo that's the problem, sir; it's those large generators in the hold. The ones for Buenos Aires. And we can't move those at sea with our equipment."

"I know." The captain puffed on his cigar, thinking. His eyes dropped to the slip of paper in his hand and then came up again. "How much of the cargo goes off in Rio? And how much in Santos?"

The mate stared at him a moment, and then smiled in sudden understanding. He dragged a thick batch of papers from his hip pocket, wet a finger, and began leafing through them. The news was good; when he looked up it was with satisfaction. "Not a great deal for either place, sir. Nothing that couldn't be shipped back from Montevideo, or even dropped off on our return, as far as that goes."

"And how about the passengers?"

"That's no problem. Three getting off in Montevideo, and the other one in Buenos Aires."

"I see." Captain Juvenal squinted thoughtfully at the end of his cigar, carefully considering the various alternatives. His eyes came up to the horizon; he frowned at it a moment and then made up his mind. The slip of paper was jammed firmly into one pocket of his sea jacket, as indicating his arrival at a decision. He nodded. "All right. We'll miss both Rio and Santos. And also the worst part of the storm. I'll make up a cable advising the company and also the Rio agents. You post a notice below."

"Right, sir," said the mate in a satisfied tone.

"And then get back to shifting that deck-cargo," the captain added dryly. "We don't intend to go to Africa to miss this storm. We'll still feel enough of it."

"Yes, sir!" said the mate with a nice combination of

alacrity and agreement, and trotted happily back down the companionway.

To the four passengers the *Santa Eugenia* carried, the change in plans made little difference; when one took a freighter one calculated the maximum travel time in any event, and none of them had plans which would be seriously inconvenienced by the changed schedule. Nor, in general, did the posted notice make any great difference to the crew. Salvador de Bahia was only two days behind them, and their pockets were empty and their vices temporarily assuaged. And, in any event, missing a storm in a ship whose cargo was out of balance was certainly no cause for any rational sailor to complain.

To one member of the crew, however, the announcement came with a shock that was sickening. As steward for the four passengers and the ship's few officers, Nacio Madeira Mendes was alone in the small dining salon when the first mate came in whistling cheerfully, thumbtacked the notice to the bit of plywood that served as bulletin board, studied his handiwork a moment and found it exceeding good, and then went back out on deck. Nacio came forward with natural curiosity to read the fatal words, interrupting his clearing of the breakfast dishes to do so. It took a few seconds for the full extent of the calamity to strike him, but when it did, the blood drained from his thin face, leaving him white and rigid with shock.

Nacio Madeira Mendes had joined the *Santa Eugenia* in Lisbon for the sole purpose of reaching his native Rio de Janeiro with the minimum of trouble. His forged passport would almost certainly have caused investigation had he traveled as a passenger by either ocean liner or airplane, since at best it was a poor job. However, it was all that Nacio had been prepared to pay for, and certainly in his opinion ample for the purposes of a dining room steward, since cabin help were always in demand and under such conditions shipping agents paid small attention to papers. And at Rio, Nacio had anticipated no difficulty at all. The crew would be given their normal shore leave, and by simply not returning to the ship he would have been free in his native land with small chance of ever being located. The false passport would have been destroyed, or possibly even sold for a profit—for the name on it was nothing likes Mendes, and the picture might easily have been of almost anyone between the ages of twelve and sixty. His jaw clenched painfully. It had all been so simple up until that moment!

Nacio Madeira Mendes was a medium-sized man, with a sharp but small beak of a nose, and a widow's peak that divided his broad forehead the slightest bit off-center. The effect was to give his lean face a rather attractive appearance, heightened somewhat by the smoothness of skin that belied his forty-two years of age. Only the coldness of his eyes, to those few who ever bothered to note them, indicated that not only was the small tense man not as young as he appeared, but that his years had not been spent in careless abandon.

As he stood swaying to the restless, creaking movement of the ship, bitter anger diffused him, flushing his face; anger at the captain for making his decision, at the storm for influencing the captain, but mostly at himself for being such an idiot. He should have jumped ship in Bahia, safely on Brazilian soil, and managed to reach Rio de Janeiro by *pau de arara,* or even by omnibus, neither of which was normally scrutinized by the police. But he had been so stupidly sure of arriving with the *Santa Eugenia* that he had wasted his time there in a ridiculous bar with a couple of even more ridiculous girls and had then staggered back like a docile imbecile to what was now going to be a prison-ship carrying him past his destination. Good God!

His thin lips pressed themselves together tightly, leaving them bloodless, as he stared at the impartial bulletin board. Sebastian had told him when they had met in Lisbon that the opportunity of a lifetime awaited him; the chance to earn a fantastic sum for a few minutes' work. And now he was being carried helplessly away from it! He tried to force down his anger and attempt a cold calculation of his position, but it was impossible. With the scheduled detour, the ship would not arrive in Montevideo for at least another four days, and Sebastian had been very clear that he had to be in Rio de Janeiro by the sixth of the month at the latest, or to forget the entire matter. And the sixth was tomorrow! Damn! And again damn! Why in the name of the beloved Saint whose job it was to watch over such fools as himself hadn't he left the ship in Salvador de Bahia?

He stood staring bitterly at the scrawled notice but in actuality only seeing the black turmoil of his thoughts. It was not until the hand on his arm had shaken him rather severely several times that he realized he was being addressed.

"Bad news, Steward?"

Even in his daze, Nacio recognized the other as being one of the four passengers, a small globular man with a full fat face and a hairline mustache curved under a tiny blob of a nose; a man named Dantas, or Dumas, or Dortas, or something like that; a man whose large black eyes were liquid and fathomless, and whose sparse graying hair seemed to have been painted in place. Nacio stared at him blankly.

"Senhor?"

The little man was patience itself. "I said, the notice seems to be somewhat of a shock to you."

"The notice?" Nacio forced his mind from the fateful meaning of the scrawled words, automatically assuming the semiservility of a steward. "No, senhor. I was merely a bit surprised. It really makes no difference to me."

The smaller man studied Nacio's features a moment thoughtfully, and then changed his tactics. His voice became conversational. "You're a Brazilian, are you not?"

It was impossible to deny this; Nacio's accent betrayed him in every word, even to this little man who spoke in a Spanish that was marked with the harsh gutturals of the Rio Plate. "A Brazilian? Yes, senhor, I am."

"And you aren't disappointed that we shall not be stopping in Rio?"

"Disappointed?" For a moment the complete inadequacy of the word almost removed Nacio's rigid control. He forced back a wave of bitterness and even managed at last to shrug, even to force a deprecating smile. "Naturally, senhor, to a Brazilian our lovely Rio de Janeiro must always be the only city in the world. And not to see it, when one is actually so close . . ."

"A pity." The tiny fathomless eyes looked at him calculatingly. "I admire you, Steward. I admire the calm way in which you accept this—ah, this disappointment." The small shoulders raised themselves delicately. "I think in your place I should be less brave."

Nacio had no choice but to fall back upon a cliché. "Senhor, in this life what one cannot overcome, one must accept." Even as he said the words, he wished he could believe them.

"Not always." The little man dropped his eyes to the worn rug of the salon a moment and then raised them. "A person of ingenuity always seeks alternate routes to his goal. Different avenues. For example," he continued evenly, "if I were you, I should still manage to get to Rio. Or at least to try." He paused a moment and then added significantly, "And I should do it today. . . ."

"Today?" Nacio studied the expression in the other's eyes a moment. The deep liquid pools seemed to be trying to give him a message, but without success. Was the little man making fun of him? The thought induced bitterness. "How, senhor? By swimming?"

"No," said the little man gently. "By becoming ill."

The faint hope that the small passenger might actually have a workable plan disappeared; it was obvious that the man was merely insane. Nor in his present mood did Nacio feel like wasting the time to humor him. "If you will please pardon me, senhor—"

The tiny hand that shot out to grasp his arm and detain him was far stronger than Nacio would have imagined.

"Ill!" said the smaller man firmly. "Sick! The captain of this ship is not the type to allow a member of his crew to suffer, and possibly to die, simply because he wishes to avoid some rough weather."

Nacio's eyes narrowed as the words of the other slowly began to germinate. It was, indeed, an idea. Possibly, even, a good idea. "But what kind of illness?"

"Appendix, I should say." The smaller man looked at him quite evenly; no trace of expression marked his full, fat face. "Now, tell the truth. You do not feel well, do you?"

Nacio studied the other carefully. "No, senhor. I do not."

"Good! I mean, I'm sorry to hear it. And, of course, you also have a terrible pain in your lower groin." Nacio's hand went automatically to his stomach. "Over a bit and a trifle lower," said the small passenger critically, and

moved Nacio's hand. He studied the effect. "That's better."

"But—"

"And nausea, of course." Dorcas—or Dantas, or Dumas, or something like that—considered the frozen face of
the steward a moment, and then nodded. "I've seen sicker
people, but I suppose it will have to do. You'd better get
to your bunk. An infected appendix can be a serious affair."

"There's just one thing—"

"I shall advise the officials." The small hand came up to
grasp Nacio's arm again, urging him toward the door. Nacio held back. It was quite obvious that this Dantas—or
Dumas or Dortas or something like that—had his own reasons for wanting the ship to dock in Rio, and was only
using him as a Judas goat. It was true that the scheme
might well serve his, Nacio's, purposes, but still . . .

"Just why are you doing this, senhor?"

"Why?" The little man smiled. "Let us say that I, too,
have suffered the pangs of homesickness, and I appreciate
them in others. Or, if you prefer, let us say that I have a
distorted sense of humor and enjoy practical jokes. Or
even, let us say," he added coldly, his smile disappearing
instantly, "that I recognize illness when I see it, and in my
estimation you should be lying down in your bunk. Now!"

His hand propelled Nacio closer to the door. The thin
steward allowed himself to be led. Regardless of the
other's motives, the fact remained that this could well be
the solution to his own problem. He assumed an expression of pain, grasped his lower groin firmly, and nodded.
"If you will pardon me, senhor . . ."

"Of course," said the small passenger pleasantly.

He looked after the departing figure of the steward a
moment thoughtfully, sighed, and then made his way to

the deck. The sky had darkened considerably, taking on a weird yellowish cast, eerie at that hour of the morning; the wind had risen, shrilling through the guy ropes of the deck cranes, heavy with the threat of coming rain. He stepped daintily across the rope-falls that snaked their way across the sloping deck, and finally located the mate. He tapped the tall young man on the shoulder a bit imperiously.

"Your steward is quite ill." His voice was raised over the wind, but still seemed to be a trifle accusing, as if the affair were somehow the mate's fault.

"Ill? The steward?"

Miguel was rather surprised to hear this particular passenger evoking any great interest in anything, let alone the health of a crew member. This one had kept to himself throughout the voyage, seldom if ever spoke at the dining table, avoided even the slight entertainment the ship offered, and was usually found at night leaning over the bow rail, staring out into the empty blackness.

"Ill," said the passenger patiently. "In great pain. It's rather obvious that the man is suffering from a badly infected appendix."

The mate stared at him a moment, shrugged, and then turned back to his work, bawling an order to the deckhands. The small passenger frowned; his voice became icy.

"Mate! Did you hear what I said? I said—"

Miguel cast his eyes toward the heavens in supplication; the growing fury there certainly offered no solution. "All right! All right!" he said with irritation. "I'll have a look at him."

He shouted out a string of orders and turned toward the bow, shaking his head in disgust. He stamped up the tilted deck, turned into a passageway, and marched angrily toward the forecastle. Stewards! And passengers! The steward had probably only been sampling the wine; or in even greater probability was only suffering from the increased roll of the ship. And with all the work to be done on deck, he had to waste time going off to hold the man's hand!

He ducked his head beneath the low portal of the forecastle and peered downward, allowing his sight to become accustomed to the dimness. A low, tortured moan came to him, intermingled with the snores of several crew members who were off duty, and also punctuated by the creaking of the ship's beams, louder and more threatening here in the confined space. The mate edged forward, frowning down at the white old-young face on the bunk. Nacio stared back. There was the rattle of a metal basin as the mate's foot inadvertently came in contact with it; the stench of vomit came to him.

"I hear you're sick. . . ."

Nacio wet his lips, speaking in a hoarse whisper. "I don't know what happened. One minute I was fine, clearing the dishes, and the next—" His pale face cringed as another spasm shook it.

Miguel's irritation drained away in an instant. This man was honestly sick; this was no result of wine-sampling, nor of *enjôo*. And as a good first mate who someday wanted to be a good master, the welfare of the crew ranked high among his responsibilities. He bent forward solicitously. "Do you have pain?"

The man in the bunk tried to raise himself on his elbows and then turned his head swiftly aside to avoid vomiting on the mate. He hung over the edge of his bunk a moment, retching violently, and then fell back. "My side . . ." One hand clutched at his lower groin on the outside of the thin cover; beneath the blanket his other hand tightly cupped the bottle of ipecac he had stolen from the dispensary." It hurts. . . ."

The first mate straightened up, studying the white face in the bunk with deep concern. "You'll be all right. Don't worry. We'll see to it. I'll be right back."

He mounted the forecastle steps thoughtfully, paused a moment to catch his balance as the ship struck an even greater roller, and then made his way through the creaking ship. This could be bad; very bad. The ship's dispensary was barely adequate for setting broken bones, or settling men's stomachs after a too-hectic shore leave, and he also knew that none of the passengers was a medical man, or at least none of them carried the title. An infected appendix could be serious trouble.

Captain Juvenal watched him climb the companionway to the bridge, recognizing in the scowl and the rigid set of the shoulders that something had happened to upset his first mate.

"What's the trouble?"

"The steward." The mate braced himself against the rail. "He's sick. I think it's his appendix. And bad."

Captain Juvenal frowned. "Are you sure?"

"Pretty sure." Miguel shook his head. "He has all the symptoms—pain in his side, and he's throwing up. . . ." He mentally scolded himself for not having checked to see if the man had a fever, but then dismissed the thought. Any man that sick obviously had to have a fever. He sighed. "He's not in good shape."

Captain Juvenal's eyes went to the black skies; clouds boiled closer, split in the distance by jagged flashes of lightning. His large hand locked to the rail, balancing himself, as he negated the first thought that had automatically come to him.

"It's no good. We still can't dock at Rio. The reports of the storm are getting worse." He rubbed the back of his hand against his bearded face wearily, thinking. "And if the man has a bad appendix and it should happen to burst . . ." He paused.

"So what do we do?"

Captain Juvenal sighed. "The only thing we can do, I suppose. We'll have to advise their coast guard—what they call their Sea Rescue Squad over here. Maybe they can be of help." He thought a moment more, spat into the ocean, and walked over, rapping sharply on the door of the radio shack. A head popped out almost instantly.

"Send a radio. To the nearest Sea Rescue Squad station; you'll find it in your book. Tell them we have a desperately sick man aboard, and we can't risk docking at Rio. Give them our coordinates and bearing and tell them—"

The mate interrupted. "It won't be easy rigging him aboard another ship in this weather."

"That's their problem. They'll know best." Captain Juvenal turned back to the waiting radioman. "Tell them we're logging between eight and ten knots, and that the seas alongside are running"—he made a rapid estimate —"five to eight meters. And tell them to hurry; the storm's getting worse. Though they should know that . . . ."

"Maybe they can send a doctor," the radioman suggested.

The captain shook his head decisively. "With the *Santa Eugenia* pitching like this? It would be a pigsticking. No. Tell them the man must be removed. And soon." He waited a moment and then glared, expending his feeling of helplessness on the innocent radioman. "Well? Well? What are you waiting for?"

The radioman, who had been waiting until he was sure the captain was finally finished, pulled his neck in, turtle-fashion, and closed the door behind him. The captain turned to the mate.

"Go down and tell the man he'll be all right. Tell him we're making arrangements to help him." His voice became crisp. "And then get back to that deck-cargo. Do you hear?"

"Yes, sir!" said the mate, and scampered down the companionway.

The crew and the passengers hung over the heaving rail of the *Santa Eugenia*, their oilskins small protection against the driving rain, but too engrossed in the drama they were watching to think of seeking shelter. Above their heads, outlined against the black sky like some prehistoric flying monster, a squat helicopter sought to hold its position while a cable snaked itself from its belly. The thin steel rope whipped back and forth, slashing at the ship's superstructure, threatening to wind itself about the deck crane rigging.

Three times the craft above was swept out of reach and had to fight itself back again, attempting to hold itself steady over the pitching deck, and also attempting to keep the cable free. Nacio, strapped tightly on a litter beneath the snapping steel cord, bit his lip and wished—not for the first time—that he had never fallen into the scheme in the first place. Cowardice was certainly not one of his vices, but the thought of being snatched from the relative safety of the deck into that terrifying sky was beyond his experience. He swallowed convulsively, fighting down an illness that had nothing to do with the ipecac, and closed his eyes, praying desperately.

There was a series of disconnected shouts, and then a sharp jerk as the cable momentarily dragged across the deck and was hastily hooked to the litter. Men stood quickly away; Captain Juvenal bent close to the shrouded figure, his beard scraping the protective tarpaulin. He spoke rapidly, well aware that another gust of wind could sweep his words away.

"You'll be all right. We'll pick you up on our return. Get in touch with the agents . . ."

Nacio opened his eyes and stared blindly up at the bearded face. I'll be all right? In that shaky little box up there? I'll be all right? A fool like me? What on earth made me think you would dock at Rio with a sick sailor? I must have been mad! Or that little man, rather, must have been mad! There was a brief tinge of satisfaction in knowing that the ends of the little passenger, whatever those ends had been, would not be served, but it was instantly wiped away as his own more immediate peril came back to him.

He closed his eyes, finding in the darkness behind his eyelids the only hope of maintaining sanity in the incredible situation. There was a series of shouted commands, echoing dimly in his ears, a sudden increase in the roar of the engine above, and then with a sickening lurch he felt himself free of the deck and twisting slowly in space. Against his will his eyes sprang open in terror; his body strained wildly against the confining straps. The litter was just clearing the rail; beneath him a gray heaving ocean reached up for him voraciously. A sheet of rain slashed his face, cold and stinging; he flinched and then opened his eyes again.

The rigid pallet paused a brief instant at the end of its short arc and then began to swing, and in that moment before the winch began sucking him upward, Nacio found himself staring into the large fathomless liquid eyes of the little passenger named Dortas—or Dumas or Dantas or something like that.

The little fat man with the round face and the hair that seemed painted in place had his face tilted upward, staring at him through the rain. It was too brief an instant to be sure, but to Nacio where there should have been some sign of disappointment in the other's expression, there was none. On the contrary, the liquid eyes were watching his agonizing ascent with what seemed to be some sort of secret amusement . . . .

Two

CAPTAIN JOSÉ MARIA CARVALHO
Santos Da Silva, liaison officer between the Brazilian police
and Interpol, braked his red Jaguar sports car to a skidding
stop and stared with a disgusted frown through the blurred
windshield. The long, narrow *entrada* that fronted the
main entrance to the Santos Dumont Airport was solidly
packed with cars. Sheets of rain whipped at the tall palms
that fronted the walk and drummed a bit impatiently on
the plastic hood of the convertible, as if demanding that the
captain get out and get soaked like everything else; the
windshield. The long, narrow *entrada* that fronted the
Brazilian negative to this idiotic suggestion. Captain Da
Silva scowled, but not because the cars parked before the
long building were in violation of the law; he was merely
expressing his envy at others luckier—and therefore
smarter—than himself who had managed to enter the
building dry.

He swiveled his head. To park in the mire of the regular parking lot on a day like this was to invite drowning, for when it rained in Rio de Janeiro, it did so with typical *Carioca* exuberance and exaggeration. And to leave the car anywhere but at the curb or in the guarded parking lot was to invite far worse. A missing carburetor, for example, or even a missing automobile. Car thieves in Rio, he recognized, were a hardy lot who were not afraid of getting drenched for a reasonable profit. And a police shield on the windshield would only make the theft more enticing, since it would guarantee the loot at least had a decent motor.

A horn behind him blared indignantly. Da Silva suddenly noted that the wide gate to the airport apron was open; he shifted gears and drove in, splashing through puddles, pulling the small car up under the shelter of a covered loading dock. An airport policeman, shocked by this disregard for rules which were certainly posted in sufficient profusion, moved over immediately from the shadow of a doorway to remonstrate, but one look at the swarthy, pockmarked face of the driver, slashed across by its flamboyant mustache and topped off by its unruly shock of black curly hair, and the policeman hastily saluted instead. Captain Da Silva at the best of times was unpredictable, but in weather like this there was a good chance he might be truly difficult. But then the seriousness of the offense—not to mention the potential consequences to his own well-being—forced the policeman to attempt a protest, although he tried to do it as diplomatically as possible.

"I'm sorry, Captain, but you really shouldn't park here. . . ."

He tilted his head in the direction of the runways. Airplanes hovered there, grounded for the moment. Their bulging sides gleamed metallically, their huge outlines were hazy in the driving rain. Beyond them across the ruffled waters of the bay the walls of Pão de Açucar rose starkly to disappear into the low-hanging clouds. The policeman's eyes returned, bright with emotion, pleading.

"This is where the catering trucks park, Captain—the ones that bring the food for the passengers. With your car in the way, they'll have to park out in the rain—"

"Good!" Da Silva bent to set his brake and then switched off the ignition. "More water, more soup." Did this cretin actually think for one moment he would inconvenience himself for the comfort of airplanes, or even for the comfort of those people foolish enough to patronize the flying monstrosities? He unfolded his mus-cular six-feet to the protected pavement and reached back into the car for his raincoat. He slung it over his arm, closed the door firmly, and then paused to pat his pocket. The letter that had been deposited on his desk a brief half-hour before was there, as mysterious and tantalizing as it had been when the Central Office of the Police had forwarded it to him as being more in his province. He pressed it again, as if for luck, and then stepped easily up to the low platform.

Against his better judgment the policeman made one last attempt. "But, Captain, sir—" One look at the fierce expression that suddenly blazed in Da Silva's eyes and he hastily swallowed the balance of his protest. "Yes, sir!"

"And you will keep an eye on it! A sharp eye," Da Silva instructed him sternly.

The policeman sighed helplessly. "Of course, Captain."

"Thank you," Da Silva said, and smiled cordially.

The policeman, amazed as were so many at how pleasant and innocuous Captain José Da Silva could appear when he chose to smile, as compared to how tough he looked—and was—when he was forced to frown, tried to return the smile, but his heart wasn't in it. One thing was positive: forcing the catering trucks to park out in the rain was no way to maintain their goodwill and hence to share in their leftovers, which was about the only decent food he and his family ever managed to get their hands on. But, on the other hand, could one of his lowly rank—or any other rank—seriously oppose Captain Da Silva? Not, he admitted sadly to himself, if one were blessed with a normal amount of the good sense.

He stared pensively out at the mottled sky and the veering sheets of rain, and prayed fervently that Captain Da Silva completed whatever errand had brought him here and then took himself and his *filho de mãe* car away before the first catering truck made its appearance. But even as he prayed he kept his eyes watchfully on the small red convertible, for all in all he was not a stupid man.

Da Silva, well aware that in all probability he had interfered in some way with one of the policeman's minor rackets—and far from crushed by the thought—walked quickly through the deserted baggage area of the Cruzeiro Do Sul, passed into a ticket area now besieged by stranded passengers and frantic clerks, ducked under the narrow counter and forced his way through the crowds that were milling about like confused geese because of the canceled schedules. He shook his head in non-understanding at their plight, came to the curved terrazzo staircase leading to the restaurant-bar on the mezzanine and trotted up it, with the disturbed buzzing of the crowd below mysteriously seeming to amplify rather than lessen as he mounted.

At the top he paused to toss his raincoat to the cloakroom attendant, patted the letter in his pocket once again, and then started through the packed room toward the familiar figure of his old friend Wilson, waiting alone at a table near the rain-streaked windows, staring pensively out at the glistening runways and the fog-shrouded bay beyond.

In appearance, Wilson was the opposite of the rugged and colorful Da Silva. There was nothing flamboyant or even particularly noticeable about the small nondescript man, and yet this anonymity was far from accidental. It was the result of years of training and served Wilson very well. On the payroll sheets that the American Ambassador was forced to initial for submittal to Washington each month, Wilson appeared as the Security Officer, a minor position mainly concerned with keeping American tourists happy and out of trouble, as well as with keeping Embassy wastebaskets empty and their contents incinerated. He was, in fact, far more important than this, as only the Ambassador alone of Embassy personnel knew. A member of several U. S. Government agencies concerned with security, he was also the only U. S. assignee to Interpol in Brazil. Da Silva was one of the very few people cognizant of Wilson's true status; he also had good reason to appreciate the ability of the mild-looking man. The two had had their share of adventures together, and in any moment of danger or crisis, Da Silva knew he would rather have the quiet American at his side than any other man he knew.

The tall Brazilian finally managed to make his way through the wedged tables with minimum damage either to himself or to the seated diners, and grinned down at his friend.

"Hi, Wilson."

"Hello, Zé."

"Sorry I'm late." It was obviously a standard gambit; Da Silva was usually late. As a Brazilian he would have considered himself unpatriotic to be early. He pulled a chair back from the table, dropping into it, and smiled apologetically. "This time, though, I have an excuse. I actually left the office in plenty of time, but what with the rain, and the traffic, and the problem of parking . . ." His bushy eyebrows rose dramatically to indicate the vastness of the problem of parking.

Wilson was studying him quizzically. For one brief second Da Silva's eyes narrowed slightly, remembering the letter in his pocket. He put the thought away and reached across the table for the bottle of Maciera Five-Star that Wilson had ordered, pouring himself a drink to match both the one before his friend as well as the one he suspected his friend had already had. He raised his glass in a small salute and made his voice casual.

"Why the odd look? Certainly not because I'm late . . ."

He took a drink, savoring it with the pleasure that always accompanied the first drink of the day, and then set his glass down. "Ah, that's better! Now, why the odd look? What happened this morning to upset you? Certainly not my tardiness. Right?"

"Right and wrong," Wilson said.

"A typical answer from an Embassy employee," Da Silva said, and grinned. "You're getting more Brazilian every day. The only thing you forgot was to qualify it with a 'perhaps.' So what happened?"

Wilson's expression didn't change. "It's true that something queer happened this morning, but that was minor. And certainly not what caused what you call my strange look."

Da Silva lit a cigarette, tossed the match in the general direction of the ashtray, pushed the package of cigarettes across the table and leaned back comfortably. "Then what did?"

"*Your* strange look."

"*My* strange look?" Da Silva looked and sounded surprised. "Is my tie crooked again? Or did I forget it all together this morning?" He glanced down a moment and then looked up again, reassured.

Wilson smiled faintly, but it was a smile that did not extend beyond his lips. "Not your tie. I mean your jacket." He tilted his head toward the large closed windows. "Even on relatively chilly days you take off your jacket the minute you arrive here for lunch; this freedom of dress is the reason you keep giving me for enduring the food here. And yet today, with the windows closed and the room stifling, you sit there with your jacket on. And even drink brandy, which certainly isn't a cooling drink."

"And you wonder why?"

"Exactly. I wonder why."

Da Silva shook his head sadly. "That's the trouble with eating lunch with a trained investigator; no secrets. Every act treated with suspicion; every motive questioned." He shrugged. "And yet, the answer is simplicity itself, although I must ask you to keep it a secret." He leaned forward conspiratorially; a waiter who had been sidling up with the intention of offering menus, backed away instantly. No one would ever be able to accuse him of eavesdropping, especially on a man he knew to be a captain of police. Da Silva peered about to make sure no one was watching, and then turned back, lowering his voice. "The truth is I have a careless laundry. My shirt has a hole in it. If it ever came out, of course, I'd be disgraced. Drummed out of the force. Stood at attention while my buttons were cut off—and believe me, my shirts are bad enough without *that!*"

"Cute," Wilson said, and then lowered his voice to match the other's. "Why don't we try this version instead? You're wearing your jacket because it would frighten the daylights out of most of the people here to see a man drinking brandy and slurping soup dressed in a shoulder holster and with the butt of a police positive swinging with every spoonful. How's that?"

Da Silva looked hurt. "Slurping soup? Me?"

"Slurping brandy, then, and drinking soup."

"That's a little better, anyway."

"And don't change the subject." Wilson's voice was unamused. "Why the armament?"

Da Silva's tone lost its light banter. He drank the balance of his brandy and reached for the bottle again. "Nothing as unimportant as you might think. It's just that for the next week or so the entire department is under orders to be constantly armed. Ridiculous—not to mention damned uncomfortable—but there it is."

Wilson studied his friend's face. "Because of the O.A.S. meeting?"

Da Silva looked surprised. "So you do read the newspapers. . . ."

"We've been alerted, of course," Wilson said, and picked a cigarette from Da Silva's pack. He lit it, inhaled deeply, and frowned at his friend through the cloud of smoke. "But I haven't felt it necessary to weigh myself down with a kilo or so of steel. Or at least not yet. After all, the meetings don't start for another week. The delegates won't start arriving before next Sunday or Monday."

"The delegates won't," Da Silva said lazily, "but we have a feeling a lot of other people have begun drifting into our fair city, some of whom might like nothing better than to use the big parade for free target practice."

His voice became deceptively innocent. "Maybe even some of your compatriots. . . ."

Wilson stared at him. "And just what is that supposed to mean?"

Da Silva shrugged. "Well, Juan Dorcas is going to be the delegate from Argentina, and as I recall he seems to take pleasure in opposing the American position on almost anything."

"And you think——?"

Da Silva looked across the table steadily. "I don't think anything. There are, however, a few things I suspect. I suspect, for example, that your C.I.A. would enjoy nothing more, shall I say, than having Senhor Dorcas come down with a severe migraine, or a rash of broken legs, and being forced to unfortunately miss these meetings. Or even worse than a rash of broken legs, perhaps . . ."

Wilson's jaw hardened. "Are you accusing us——?"

Da Silva looked bland. "My dear Wilson, I'm not accusing you of anything. I'm merely stating a fact. And if your conscience bothers you because of your past history in similar cases—a list I'm sure you're even more familiar with than I am—then I'm sorry."

Wilson stared at him a moment and then crushed out his cigarette. He reached for the bottle. "If it will help," he said quietly, "let me assure you on my word as your friend that nothing like this is being planned, not even faintly."

"As far as you know."

"As far as I know. And I would know."

Da Silva grinned. "Wilson, I love you. And, within certain limits, I trust you. But, if I were in your shoes, and I were under instructions from Washington, I'd also be circumspect." He held up a hand to prevent interruption. "Also, if I were the head of C.I.A. sitting up in

Washington and planning something, I doubt if I would put out a mimeographed release of all my plans. Not even to every member of the C.I.A."

"In other words," Wilson said slowly, "you wouldn't believe me no matter what I said."

"I wouldn't go that far," Da Silva said, "but I admit, in this case, that I'd come pretty close." He put out his cigarette and smiled. "In any event, it's my job to cover all the angles. Even as you would do if this meeting were taking place in Washington. After all, it's our basic responsibility not to have anything happen. If this meeting were taking place in Washington, you'd probably be walking around with guns in every pocket, and a cutlass between your teeth."

Wilson tried to simmer down. He took a deep breath and forced himself to take a light tone to equal Da Silva's. "Not me," he protested. "My dentist wouldn't permit it. Besides, I'm the peaceful type."

"Now, that's where I'm different," Da Silva said, and sighed. "I'm the curious type. For example, I'm curious to know why people don't stay home." He raised one large hand quickly. "Not tourists, of course—which we desperately need—but diplomats, at least. It seems to me that it would be a lot more diplomatic remaining in one's own capital than endangering foreign relations by being stoned, or spat upon, or being shot at. And, of course, it would leave a lot of policemen time for a few other chores, like handling the already overloaded docket."

Wilson tried to go along with the concept. "You mean no more international meetings? A return to the sixteenth century?"

Da Silva shook his head. "On the contrary. I mean moving into the enlightened twentieth century. After all, scientists sweated blood to develop satellites and closed television—why not use these technical advances logically? Why not use closed television for these meetings? That way everyone could stay at home in front of his own fireplace. It seems to me to be a lot more practical use of the invention than simply showing the Easter Parade on Fifth Avenue to natives of Zanzibar, or running off old cowboy movies for the confusion of eighteen races." He thought a moment. "Including yours, of course. . . ."

"It's really not a bad idea," Wilson conceded, "although I can think of a few objections."

Da Silva frowned at him indignantly. "Name one!"

"Well," Wilson said slowly, fingering his glass, "suppose one of the delegates didn't like what another one was saying. He might just reach across and switch off the set."

Da Silva stared at him. "And you consider this a disadvantage?"

Wilson grinned, his past irritation forgotten. "Well, maybe not. A far greater disadvantage, of course, is that under that system, how would we get rid of counterpart funds? And can you imagine the uproar in Congress if none of the public's money was used for junkets abroad? Why, you might even balance the budget! And you'd definitely put the airlines out of business in a week. Not to mention two thousand clerks in the General Accounting Office."

"That's true," Da Silva conceded, and grinned. "It wouldn't bother me greatly to put the airlines out of business, but I'd hate to think of the blow to the United States economy if two thousand clerks were let loose on the streets of Washington all at one time."

"Two thousand more, you mean," Wilson said.

"Plus eighty C.I.A. agents," Da Silva added innocently.

Wilson's smile faded abruptly. "You're still on that kick, are you? Will you please accept the fact that the C.I.A.—"

"—is a fine organization full of dedicated men with excellent ideals and good profiles," Da Silva ended. He smiled. "Unfortunately, not particularly interested in Brazilian problems, which is what I have to worry about." His smile faded. "In any event, we've rounded up as many of our own bad boys as we could find—or recognize —and we've got the docks and the airports covered pretty thoroughly. We've picked up a couple of men who might have caused some trouble, but I'm sure we haven't gotten them all."

Wilson looked at him sardonically. "And none of them Americans?"

"No," Da Silva admitted, "but that doesn't impress me too much. Now that you've exported chewing gum and sunglasses and Hollywood shirts around the world it's pretty hard to tell an American from a native. And also, of course," he added with a faint smile, "people— who I won't name—have been known to hire local talent to do their chores for them."

Wilson shook his head hopelessly. "Once you get an idea in your head, Zé, it's hard to reason with you. As far as Juan Dorcas is concerned, there have been other attempts to get him before this. Now, I suppose, you'll claim they were all the work of the C.I.A."

"No." Da Silva looked at him steadily. "Not all of them. Maybe none of them. Feelings run pretty high in some of these countries down here; diplomats sometimes speak for their governments and sometimes don't—but they seldom speak for the people. And often when they do it's for the wrong reasons. And people being what they are, it's not uncommon to try and solve problems the quickest way. But no matter who may want to solve the problem of Juan Dorcas, our job is to see to it they don't. At least not here in Brazil." He sighed. "I'll be a lot happier when these O.A.S. meetings are over."

"I can well imagine," Wilson said with pretended sympathy. "You won't have to dream up your wild cloak-and-dagger ideas out of your head—you can go back to getting them from the TV." He snorted. "Dorcas! He must be some sort of a nut!"

Da Silva contemplated him curiously. "What makes you say that? Have you ever seen the man? Or talked to him?"

"No," Wilson admitted. "I don't think I've even seen a good, recognizable photograph of him. I understand he doesn't like newspapermen, or photographers."

"And in your opinion that makes him some sort of a nut?"

Wilson refused to be drawn in by the gentle sarcasm. "That's not the reason. The man's supposed to be fantastically wealthy, with large investments in almost every South American country—"

Da Silva nodded evenly. "That's true."

"—and yet," Wilson continued, "he opposes every move our Government makes to try and hold off revolutions in these countries. Even though he'd be the first to lose everything if any Government came in that followed even the most minor form of expropriation. In my opinion, *that* makes him some sort of a nut."

Da Silva shook his head slowly. "You know, Wilson," he said at last, "this may be hard for you to accept, but not everyone agrees with the means your Government takes to combat revolution. In fact, some people think your means actually fosters it." He shrugged. "Dorcas happens to be one of them."

"Fosters it? You're crazy!"

"Am I? Maybe. On the other hand, to take one small example, when you people went into the Dominican Republic, you did so on the basis of a claim from your diplomats there that there were some eighteen—or maybe the figure was twenty-eight, or possibly even thirty-eight—active Communists there that constituted a threat to democratic government there—"

Wilson frowned at him. "And you don't believe there were?"

"I'm sure there were," Da Silva said gently. "In fact, knowing the accuracy of diplomatic reports, I'm sure there were more. My point is, however, after you were there awhile, the figure probably jumped to a hundred times that number. That, my friend, is what the word 'fosters' means." He held up a hand to prevent Wilson from breaking in. "Now, if I were Senhor Dorcas, interested in protecting my investments, I'm afraid I'd at least take a good, long look at any method that resulted in an increase in revolutionary feeling on that scale."

Wilson stared at him. "And so, in your opinion, we should simply do nothing?"

Da Silva suddenly grinned. "In my opinion I shouldn't be giving you my opinion. It serves no purpose for me, and I'm sure it won't change your ideas in the slightest." His grin faded. "I suppose you do what you feel you have to do. Which, after all, is exactly what Juan Dorcas does. And what I do as far as preventing trouble for my country." He leaned back, his black eyes studying his friend, his strong fingers twisting the stem of his brandy glass. "Well, enough of politics. We've been fortunate to avoid the subject in the past; let's leave it that way."

Wilson looked into the dark eyes across from him for several moments and then nodded. "Fair enough. As long as you don't get carried away by any wild worries about the C.I.A."

Da Silva grinned. "How about the O.G.P.U.? Have I your permission to worry about them?"

Wilson started to frown and then broke down and laughed. "You're impossible! All right, worry about whomever you want to worry about."

"That's better," Da Silva said. He reached for the cigarettes and drew one out, lighting it. "Now, what was this queer thing that happened to you this morning? This queer, but minor, thing?"

"Fancy your still remembering!" Wilson said with exaggerated admiration. "After your romantic flights of fancy, though, I'm afraid you'll find it a pretty dull story."

"I like dull stories," Da Silva said. "What happened?"

"Well," Wilson said, leaning back in his chair, "if you must know, it was something that happened at the hospital just before I came here this noon. You know I'm one of the trustees of the Stranger's Hospital—which is one of the penalties for being a foreign resident in this town who can't think up evading excuses fast enough—and this morning we had one of our endless meetings, and . . ." He paused, as if to put his words into proper order.

"And found out you were broke?"

Wilson grinned. "That, too, but there's certainly nothing unusual about that. Or minor, either; but I'll discuss that aspect with you on our next fund drive."

"I'm sure. So what happened?"

"Well," Wilson continued with a slight frown, "after the meeting was over and we were getting ready to break up for lunch, someone came in to tell us we had lost a patient. . . ."

Da Silva's smile disappeared; sympathy appeared in his eyes. "Lost a patient? Who was he? How did he die?"

Wilson shook his head. "Not that. No. It seems we actually *lost* a patient." He spread his hands. "Lost, like the opposite of found."

"How do you lose a patient?" Da Silva stared at him curiously. "I can't even see how you could misplace one, with the fabled efficiency of the Americans and English who run Stranger's Hospital."

"The operative word there is 'fabled,'" Wilson explained. "What happened in this particular case was that one of the ambulances was called out on an emergency—a serious appendix case as I understand it—and they picked the man up, all right, and stashed him neatly in the rear, all right; only when they got back to the hospital and went to drag him out—what do you know?" He shrugged humorously. "No patient."

"No patient?"

"That's right. I suppose the man became frightened at the thought of having somebody cut into him, and—"

Da Silva frowned across the table. "A man with a bad appendix attack calls an ambulance and then changes his mind halfway to the hospital? A bit unusual, isn't it?"

"I said it was queer," Wilson said patiently. "Anyway, that's the story. He must have gotten out of the ambulance when it stopped for a traffic light, or something."

Da Silva stared at him and shook his head. "In this downpour? Not to mention the fact that the thought of an ambulance anywhere in the world—but especially in Rio de Janeiro—stopping for a traffic light is ridiculous. Or for anything else, for that matter. The only reason they stop for stone walls is that they haven't figured out yet how to go through them." He nodded confidently. "But they will. I'm sure it's only a question of time."

"Well," Wilson said reasonably, "I'm sure he didn't step out when it was screaming around corners at ninety miles an hour." He raised his shoulders and smiled. "Or maybe the attendants stopped somewhere for a *cafezinho*. It wouldn't surprise me. After all, it was only supposed to be an emergency."

Da Silva looked at him. "But doesn't one of the attendants usually ride in back with the patient?"

"Not in weather like this," Wilson said. "It takes two up front. One to drive and the other to try to keep the windshield wipers going."

"I'm serious."

"So am I. If you want to loan us a good mechanic from the police garage, we'll accept."

Da Silva shook his head. "Do the police know about this? I don't mean your windshield wipers. . . ."

Wilson nodded. "They know. The police sergeant stationed in the emergency ward was there when the ambulance came back. But I don't imagine they'll waste too much time looking for a man who doesn't want to come to the hospital. We're busy enough with those that do." He shrugged lightly. "In any event, we'll be able to recognize the poor devil when and if we ever do find him."

"How?"

Wilson grinned. "In this weather? He'll be the bad appendix case also suffering from double pneumonia."

"Or flat feet, if he jumped," Da Silva said dryly, and glanced at his wristwatch. "Good Lord! Look at the hour!" He crushed out his cigarette and began getting to his feet. "Let's get the check and get out of here. I've got a busy afternoon ahead of me."

"The check?" Wilson stared at him. "We haven't eaten yet!"

"We haven't—?" Da Silva slowly settled back into his chair and then turned to wave at a waiter. "We haven't, have we?" He shook his head, but only half-humorously. "I really *will* be glad when these O.A.S. meetings are over. If I can't remember whether or not I've eaten, I'm getting in sad shape."

"Don't worry about it," Wilson said soothingly, and pushed the bottle of brandy across the table. "Take a drink and relax. It's easily explained. It's simply because you're sitting here with your jacket on. You always put it back on when you're finished eating and ready to leave, so naturally, finding yourself properly clothed, you automatically assumed—"

"The art of deductive reasoning, eh?" Da Silva said, and grinned.

Wilson shrugged modestly.

"Now, if I were you," Da Silva said, pouring his glass half full, "I'd save my deductive genius for figuring out why a sick man with a bad appendix would call an ambulance and then jump out of it on the way to a hospital. . . ." His tone was light, but there was a serious look in his dark eyes.

"Oh, I've already done that," Wilson said airily.

"You have?"

"Of course." Wilson's eyes twinkled; he leaned forward confidentially. "I did it while you were pouring that last drink. Actually, the man didn't get out at all, or at least not of his own volition."

"I see." Da Silva nodded. "You mean he was kidnapped."

"No," Wilson said. "The way I figure it, the attendants didn't want to admit they were speeding, but what actually happened was that they took a curve too fast and our patient simply went flying—"

"In this weather?" Da Silva shook his head. "He couldn't go flying. The runways are closed."

"Flying without runways. Flying under one's own power.

It has to be." He looked at Da Silva in a superior manner. "Once you have eliminated the impossible, whatever remains, however improbable, must be the truth." He shrugged modestly. "Just a little thing I coined together with a friend of mine named Doyle."

He had expected a smile from his friend, but instead Da Silva was looking at him in a curious manner. "The only question, of course," the tall Brazilian said slowly, "is what is impossible."

"That's easy," Wilson said, and leaned back in his chair. "Your suspicions about the C.I.A. and your friend Dorcas, for instance. Those are impossible."

Da Silva said nothing; instead his jaw tightened slightly. His hands slid into his jacket pockets; one hand stroked the envelope there. Wilson studied the serious look on his friend's face and then became equally serious.

"I have a feeling, Zé, that there's something you're not telling me. . . ."

Da Silva's fingers tightened on the smooth envelope. It had arrived from Salvador de Bahia that morning addressed to the Security Division of the Foreign Office, and had only filtered through the system to arrive at his desk a few moments before he had left for lunch. It had been written in a small angular hand, had been both unsigned and undated. Its message was extremely succinct:

> *Juan Dorcas will be assassinated at the coming O.A.S. meetings. I leave it to your judgment which nation stands to gain the most by his death.*

Da Silva studied his friend's face evenly.

"I have a feeling," he said slowly, "that there's probably a lot neither one of us is telling the other. . . ." And he turned rather abruptly to give his order to the small waiter standing patiently at their side.

Three

IN THE LATTER YEARS of the nineteenth century, the center of social activity in the then relatively small city of Rio de Janeiro was centered for the most part about the picturesque arches of the section called Lapa, at the juncture of the Rua Riachuelo, Mem de Sá, and the rest of the spider web of minor streets that also sought haven in the friendly atmosphere of the gay *praça*. In those days, many who preferred not to live too far away were forced by the configuration of the neighborhood to build their two-storied stucco homes on the rocky shelves that jutted from the *serra* above, and in many cases to join them with the winding Rua Riachuelo far below with ladderlike streets of granite steps, unmountable by the hansom cabs and fiacres of the day, or even by the high bicycles which were slowly beginning to gain favor among the more affluent.

Today, the *Carioca*, bound by the imagined necessity of living only where one may be delivered by automobile or omnibus, has abandoned these narrow climbing defiles to those hardy souls too poor to afford mechanical transportation, or to those few aesthetics who consider the low rental and excellent view worth the effort of getting home. And, of course, a few who fall into neither of these categories also live here, for the towering heights of the *morro* are seldom visited by strangers—such as police—since the climb is a long and arduous one.

Nacio Madeira Mendes, slowly making his way from one wide slippery step to the next up the steep Ladeira Portofino, had long since ceased to protect himself against the gusts of driving rain that had soaked him to the skin seconds after he had left the ambulance. His only hope was that Sebastian was at home, and had a change of dry clothing available, as well as a bottle of something warming, be it cognac, or even *pinga*. The water rushing down the incline of the granite steps swirled madly about his sodden shoes and several times nearly took him off balance. He paused momentarily to catch his breath and glance about, bracing himself against the onslaught of the torrent, and wiped his face more from force of habit than from any hope of benefit to be gained from the action. Below him the red tile roofs glistened wetly; across the stepped and tilted roofs the buildings of downtown Rio were lost in the gray mist of the driving rain.

He shook his head. The pleasure he had always thought to experience upon returning to his beloved Rio de Janeiro after an absence of nearly three years was oddly missing; in his dreams he had somehow always pictured himself coming back on a day when the hot sun would be gleaming from the deep blue of the sea, and when warm winds would be ruffling the giant palm trees, lifting their fronds in welcoming gestures. It was not that he hadn't remembered how it could rain in Rio—*Deus me livre*, how it could rain!—but it was only that somehow he had been sure he would come back on a day of good weather, and as a result felt a bit cheated. And even the slight pleasure of having outwitted a seemingly impossible situation by escaping the *Santa Eugenia* no longer gave him the feeling of calculated elation he had allowed himself once the helicopter was descending at Galeão Airport and he realized he was not going to be destroyed in the flimsy craft after all. If any pleasure could be garnered from the events of the morning at all, it could only have been when he managed to leave the ambulance, and this mainly because he had been sure at any moment they would skid into a lamp-post, and that both he and the two maniacs in front would be crushed to bits.

The escape from the ambulance had been much easier than he had anticipated. He had been sitting in the back of the vehicle—for he had not tolerated lying down once his restrictive straps were removed—wondering at what point he should hammer on the front panel and get them to stop, when the ambulance had come roaring into the Frei Caneca to encounter a solid line of trucks trapped behind a stalled omnibus. Fortunately, the driver of the ambulance had managed to halt his careening charge in time. Even more fortunately he had jumped down to answer the reflections on his ancestry offered by one of the truck drivers who wearied of hearing a siren keen in his ear when he obviously was helpless to get out of the way. The ambulance driver had instantly been joined by his helper, who resented trucks and their drivers as a matter of medical principle, since he felt they prevented ambulances from attaining their true and predestined velocity. During the argument Nacio simply got out, closed the doors behind him, and moved swiftly around the nearest corner. No one saw him. The few people who were on the street at the moment were scurrying along with their heads bent against the rain, in no position to observe anything but their shoes, or the potholes in the sidewalk.

Nacio sighed, staring up at the apparently endless steps still waiting to be climbed, and then resumed his dreary march. One thing was certain; the job that Sebastian had for him had better be worth all the trouble and discomfort he had suffered. He was referring, of course, to the fee he would receive, and not to the nature of the assignment, for this had not only been understood, but had also been discussed in Lisbon. In any event, anyone who employed Nacio Madeira Mendes did so for one reason only, and that was to utilize the one true talent he possessed. There was nobody in Brazil, interior or urban, more accurate with a high-powered rifle than he; and extremely few with less compunction as to where it was aimed.

The broad steps narrowed as they neared the summit, as if the builders had tired of dragging the heavy slabs up the hill, and had also realized that the traffic at that level did not warrant any more labor than was necessary. Nacio managed the last of them and turned wearily into the semi-protection of the doorway to the last house on his left. Beyond him the thick *matto* of the mountain ran up to a spur and then disappeared in the eerie fog of the rain.

He pushed at the bell for several moments before the darkness of the house struck him; his head swiveled sharply, almost animal-like, in sudden concern that Sebastian might be away and that his long climb had been in vain. But then he saw the flicker of a candle behind the heavy curtains of the house below, and a sigh of relief escaped him. It was only one of the periodic breakdowns in the services of the Companhia de Light, probably caused by the storm, or by an engineer pushing the wrong button. For some reason this assurance that his native city had not changed in his absence did nothing to soothe him; he withdrew his hand from the bell and pounded on the door instead, taking some of his pent-up frustration out on the peeling panel.

There was a slight twitch of a curtain at an upper window, and a few moments later the door opened to the restricted gap allowed by a chain bolt. In the opening an attractive girl in her late twenties stood, one hand behind her, as if demonstrating the possibility of a weapon for protection. Her large dark eyes took in the sodden figure, and then glanced down the deserted steps of the Ladeira before returning to his face warily. She pushed her thick hair back from her face, satisfied that this visitor offered no threat, unconsciously taking a slightly coquettish posture. Her voice was low and musical, although still slightly cautious. Visitors at this height were rare.

"Yes? What do you want?"

"Senhor Pinheiro. Is he in?"

She studied him a moment. "He's sleeping."

Nacio glowered, exploding. "Well, damn it, wake him up!" In the name of the sixteen saints blessed to Rio, was he expected to travel halfway around the globe and then stand out in a driving rain until Sebastian finished his beauty nap?

If he had hoped to impress the girl by either the harshness of his tone or the scowl on his face, he failed completely. There was a slight withdrawal in her appearance, but her black eyes continued to study his face with no expression at all.

"Wake him for whom?"

"Tell him that Nacio—" Nacio's eyes narrowed a bit, flickering over the girl, over the empty doorway behind her, as if assessing every potential danger. "Tell him it's a friend of his. From Lisbon." A gust of wind drove water against the thin cover of his shirt; despite his intention to appear tough before this girl, he winced. "And tell him to hurry!"

"*Momento.*" The door closed slowly but firmly in his face.

He jammed his hands into his trouser pockets and hunched his shoulders against the rain, staring bitterly down past the stepped red roofs. Far below, hazy in the rain, a car passed the entrance to the Ladeira, sheets of water spraying from its wheels. He shook his head angrily. What a day to come home! What a miserable day to come home! And how could the warm rain of Rio that he remembered so well manage to chill so unaccountably? And, even more important, what in the devil was keeping Sebastian?

There was a more prolonged wait this time, and then at last the door was eased back slowly, suspiciously, and then hastily relaxed to allow the chain bolt to be removed. A heavyset, handsome man in his late thirties stood in the doorway, brown hair tousled. Astonishment fought with sleepiness on his fleshy face.

"Nacio! How in the devil—?" Sebastian seemed to realize at last that it was raining, and that not only his guest but he, himself, could get wet. "But get in here first!"

The soaked man pushed himself brusquely across the threshold, disdaining the proffered hand; Sebastian paused to peer down the empty granite steps—it was apparently an ingrained habit—and then slammed the door and reset the chain. He turned to the girl, standing quietly and watchfully to one side.

"Iracema! Some candles from the kitchen! And a drink of something warm!" He turned back, reaching out, taking the other by the arm. "Nacio! You made it! I never expected . . ."

Nacio shrugged himself loose from the unwelcome hand and looked about the dim room as if determining upon which chair he might discard his wet clothing. Sebastian for some reason seemed to understand this vague gesture.

"And get out of those wet clothes. Iracema! A robe—" It occurred to him that the soaked man might easily cause one of his robes to shrink, or to fade. "Or better yet, a blanket." He turned back to the waiting Nacio; the thin man's lips were curled, as if he could read the other's mind. "Get out of those wet clothes. All we need at this point is for you to get sick."

Nacio smiled grimly. "Don't worry about me. If I haven't gotten sick listening to you for the past few minutes, I'll never get sick."

Sebastian chose to disregard the comment. "Get out of them anyway." He nodded as another thought struck him. "And don't worry about Iracema. She's seen men before."

"I'm sure." Nacio peeled off his shirt and followed it with his clinging trousers. The girl appeared from the stairway, walking with an even sway, carrying a folded blanket; she placed it on a chair and left the room for the candles. With the barest turn to allow himself to remove his underclothes with some semblance of privacy, Nacio wrapped himself in the blanket. Its soft weight felt good. He turned to face Sebastian. "And how about that drink?"

"The drink? Oh, yes, the drink. Iracema—"

The girl was already returning, her full hips moving sensuously, her large breasts a lush promise behind her loose sweater. One hand dangled a bottle; the other carried several candles. Sebastian bent to provide glasses from a sideboard as the candles were lit; the girl came forward, poured the drinks, and then stood back. Nacio eyed her calm beauty with inner wonder that a person like Sebastian had ever manged to get a girl like that, and then dismissed the thought, sinking into a chair. There was a time and a place for everything, and the present moment was not for girls. Right now the time was for doing the job and getting paid for it. If the fee were decent, he could have all the girls he wanted. He sipped his drink and felt the headiness of the raw *pinga* ease away the last vestiges of his weariness.

"Ah . . . that's better!"

Sebastian was frowning at him. "I'm certainly glad you made it, but how the devil you did I can't imagine."

Nacio looked at him with a curiosity suddenly tinged with suspicion. "Why all the surprise? You're the one who came to Lisbon and—" He stopped abruptly, his narrowed eyes moving to lock themselves on the silent girl.

Sebastian smiled faintly. "It's all right. You can talk in front of Iracema."

"I'm sure." Nacio's cold eyes hardened. "But I won't."

Sebastian's smile faded. "I said you can talk in front of her. She knows who you are and why you're here."

Nacio's face froze. For a moment it appeared as if anger might explode, but then his expression became calculating as he studied the girl. She watched him evenly, as one watches an inanimate object, curious, but not particularly interesting. Nacio swirled the liquid in his glass a bit and then nodded.

"All right," he said at last, slowly. "We have to start this discussion someplace, and I suppose that's as good a place to start as any. Iracema knows why I'm here? Good. Now suppose you tell me."

Sebastian shook his head. "First I want to know how you got here. I understood you were coming on the *Santa Eugenia,* and I've been checking on it every day." He tossed his shot of *pinga* down his throat, grimaced at its harshness, and handed the empty glass to the girl for refilling, wiping his mouth on the back of his hand. "This morning I found out she wasn't stopping in Rio."

He took the replenished glass from the girl and dropped into a chair across from the watchful Nacio. Iracema came to sit on the arm of his chair, resting one hand lightly on his shoulder. Nacio studied her face; there seemed to be something almost maternal in the glance she was giving Sebastian; Nacio's lip curled. The heavyset man drank and laid aside his glass. "And it's just as well she didn't dock. . . ."

Despite the soothing narcosis of the liquor a slow burning anger began to grow in Nacio. Just as well the ship didn't dock? Just as well for whom? Maybe just as well for this overstuffed middleman of crime, too cowardly to do his own killing, sitting here in comfort with his overblown girl friend, while he had had to suffer to make it to shore. Some of the anger showed in his voice.

"What do you mean, just as well?"

"Just what I say." Sebastian frowned at him, not understanding why Nacio appeared irritated. "I mean that every ship that has docked in Rio these past few days—freighter or passenger liner—has been checked by the police from one end to the other. I mean if you had been aboard her and the *Santa Eugenia* had docked here, you would almost certainly be in the hands of the police right now."

Nacio stared at him blankly, his anger disappearing. Sebastian nodded. "That's right. So how did you get here?"

A slightly wolfish smile touched Nacio's thin lips. "By the *Santa Eugenia*." He shrugged. "When I found out they weren't docking, I managed to get sick—sick enough so that the captain arranged to have me taken off the ship. By helicopter." His grin widened. "Very simple."

Sebastian shook his head slowly. "You were born with the luck of a seventh son. Let's just hope you stay lucky."

"Don't worry about my luck." Nacio reached over for the bottle, poured himself another drink, and tossed it down. He considered the bottle a moment and then placed it at arm's length from the chair, as if indicating that the time for relaxation was over. "Anyway I'm here. So what's the job? And regardless of what Iracema knows or doesn't know, I still prefer to talk business with you alone."

Sebastian leaned forward. "I told you before that Iracema knows about you and about the deal. In fact, she insisted on knowing all about you before she agreed to work with you."

"Work with *me?*" The smaller man's cold eyes became even colder. "I work alone. You know that."

"Not on this job," Sebastian said calmly. "On this job you work with Iracema. Because it's necessary to the whole plan."

"Then change the plan! I work alone." His tone was flat. "And if I ever do work with anyone else, it won't be a woman."

Sebastian studied the thin tense face calculatingly. The larger man was well aware of the potential dynamite stored up in his smaller companion, but he was also aware that for the job he had been commissioned to complete, nobody could do it as well as Nacio Mendes.

"Listen to me, Nacio. This is the biggest thing I've ever had a hand in. This thing has been planned to the last—"

"I don't care how it's been planned." Nacio's lips twisted slightly and then straightened. "I still work alone."

The larger man took a deep breath. "Then I'm sorry, but you're out." He raised a fleshy hand, forestalling any immediate reply. "I'm sorry, but there's too much at stake here, and far too much money involved to change any plans now."

Nacio's eyes narrowed; an argument from Sebastian was

something he had never expected. The big florid man was a coward, and Nacio knew it. And was also aware that Sebastian knew it. He suspected with a sudden touch of insight that the girl also knew it, but that for some unaccountable reason found this one of the man's attractions. Well, whatever the motives, Nacio had no intention of changing his methods. He relaxed, shrugging.

"And where does that leave me?"

"Just where you are." Sebastian seemed to be relieved that there had been no outburst. He spread his hands, but his eyes remained sharp. "In Rio, where you wanted to be, and at my expense, if I may remind you. And with no obligations." He turned his head to the girl on the chair arm. "So I guess we'll have to go into Nova Iguaçu after all, *querida,* and talk with Pedroso. . . ."

The smaller man across from him smiled sneeringly at this transparent attempt to intrigue him. "Pedroso? He couldn't hit the deck of a ship if somebody dropped him off the bridge."

"He could hit the man I want him to hit," Sebastian said evenly, turning back. "And that's all that counts. And he'll work with Iracema, and follow orders. And that also counts."

Nacio sneered. "Fair enough. You've just hired yourself João Pedroso. Good luck to all three of you. I'll see you in jail." He reached out and retrieved the bottle, pouring himself another drink. He raised it in a sardonic toast and then paused. "Just for the record, though, how much money did I talk myself out of?" His eyes were mocking the pair across from him. "In Lisbon you kept talking about how big the job was, but you never did get around to mentioning figures."

For a moment a cruel gleam of satisfaction came into the heavy man's face. Beside him, Iracema's breath quickened a bit. "Just for the record," Sebastian said softly, "just so you appreciate the situation, you just talked yourself out of twenty million cruzeiros. . . ."

There were a few moments of dead silence.

"That's right," Sebastian said quietly. "Twenty thousand conto."

Nacio set his full glass carefully on the floor and sat back again, his eyes sharp on the other's face. Sebastian never joked with him. He glanced at the girl and then back again. "All right. Who is it? What's the deal?"

"No deal," Sebastian said and shrugged a trifle elaborately. "Unless, of course, you're willing to work with Iracema."

The smaller man waved this aside with the contempt it deserved. "You know better than that. For twenty thousand conto I'd work with the devil. What's the deal?" He frowned, considering. "Who's worth that much dead? Or at least twice that much, since you never take less than half?" His eyes narrowed further. "And who's paying? Who's paying that much money to have someone killed?"

Sebastian shook his head. "As to your victim, you'll be told at the proper time. As for the principal? You'll never be told."

Nacio accepted this; the identity of the principal was one he rarely knew, and one that never meant any more money in his pocket in any event. But the victim? "Why not the name of the victim now?"

"Because," Sebastian said evenly, "if anything should go wrong, or if the police should recognize you and pick you up—beforehand—the less you know the better. Because the scheme wouldn't stop. It might mean Pedroso, or even another, but the scheme wouldn't stop."

Nacio nodded. It was a logical answer and one he was prepared to also accept. Twenty thousand conto! A fortune! Even translated to dollars, accepting the miserable exchange of the day, it was over twenty-two thousand dollars, far above any fee he had ever dreamed of! He recalled once when he had killed for as little as five.

"All right," he said quietly. "What's the plan?"

Sebastian took a deep breath. So far everything had gone pretty much as he had anticipated, and he wanted to be sure and explain things quite clearly, so that they would continue to go as he anticipated.

"Listen and listen carefully," he said slowly. "To begin with, next week the Organization of American States— the O.A.S.—has meetings scheduled in Rio. Delegates from all the countries of the Americas will be here; ambassadors, foreign ministers, secretaries of state—" He spread his hands impressively to indicate the importance of the delegates, and then dropped them flatly to his knees. His eyes were fixed on Nacio's face with a slight glitter, but his voice remained steady. "One of these people will be your target. . . ."

If he had expected any reaction he was bound to be disappointed; no muscle moved on Nacio's face. Obviously the affair was more than a simple husband-wife disagreement, or a falling out of partners. At those prices it had to be something of this size.

"Go on."

"All right." Sebastian bent even closer; Iracema's hand moved almost tenderly along his arm. "The first day of the meetings, before they start their actual work, there are going to be ceremonies. The meetings are planned for the Hotel Gloria, where most of the delegates will be staying, but before they begin there is going to be a motorcade to the War Memorial, where they plan to place a wreath, and from there they'll be going on to the *Municipal*, where some other ceremony is being planned. Now—"

Nacio frowned. "And how do you know all this?"

"By reading the newspapers," Sebastian said with a faint smile. The smile disappeared instantly. "Let me finish. The man who will be your target will be in prominence both in the motorcade and at the War Memorial. The best time to do the job will be during the wreath-laying ceremony, or just before. They'll be in open cars—"

"Unless it rains," Nacio pointed out. "Like it did today."

"If it rains they may not be in open cars, but they'll still get out for the wreath-laying ceremony. And that's when you'll take him."

Nacio thought a moment. "When does all this take place?"

"On Tuesday, a week from tomorrow."

Nacio sat up in growing anger; a flush began to suffuse his sallow face. "So what was the big rush in my getting here by tomorrow? I could have stayed with the *Santa Eugenia* until she docked in Montevideo and still have been here in plenty of time!"

Sebastian shook his head. "Not according to the plan, and that's what we're all going to live by." He leaned closer. "Listen closely; there is no doubt the police will be checking out the buildings along the route of this motorcade; a routine check, but it can still be thorough. They'll check out both apartments and office buildings, or at least as many of them as they can. And they'll have people stationed on the roofs as well as in the motorcade itself, and in the crowds—"

Nacio watched the heavy face across from him. "Why all the precautions? Are they expecting something?"

"No. Or at least not that I know of. But ever since Dallas—" Sebastian shrugged. "At any rate, we have to be prepared for them doing it. So as you can see it won't be as easy as some of the other jobs I've fixed you up with in the past. On the other hand, it wouldn't pay this kind of money if it were simple. In any event, the job still shouldn't be too hard, despite all their precautions. Because"— a faint smile spread across his face—"you're going to be in the Serrador Hotel, on the eighth floor, facing the Beira Mar and the War Memorial, and you're going to be using a very fine rifle with a very high-powered telescopic sight. . . ."

The smaller man's jaw tightened. "And you think they won't check hotels?"

"Of course they'll check hotels." Sebastian's smile became a bit disdainful. "But they'll pay the most attention to people who register in the last day or two before the meetings—and you have a reservation for tomorrow, a full week early. Which, of course, is why it was necessary for you to be here early." His smile broadened, proud of the attention to detail which had gone into his plan. "And the police will also check most carefully on single people, and mainly men; and you are registered there"—his voice dropped to permit his full genius to be appreciated—"as Dr. and Senhora Carabello of Três Rios."

"Senhora?"

"Iracema." Sebastian looked at him quietly. "As man and wife, but only for the purposes of the scheme. And let me repeat that and save you from any mistaken ideas you might get. For your information, Iracema and I—" He cleared his throat, breaking off the discussion as being irrelevant. "In any event you have a reservation for tomorrow, and I have proper luggage for you here. Proper clothes and everything else you'll need. So everything is set as far as that part of the plan is concerned."

"And that's why Iracema is involved?"

"Partly. I'll tell you about the rest later. Now—"

"And who's paying for all this?"

"Someone who can afford it, believe me." He waved off further interruption. "The most important thing, of course, is this: how accurate can you be at that distance?"

Nacio tugged the blanket about his lean body and closed his eyes, picturing in his mind the Serrador Hotel, the War Memorial, and the distances involved. His eyes opened slowly; he nodded. "If it's a good rifle and a good telescopic sight, there should be no problem. Depending, of course, on how open the target happens to be."

"He'll be open," Sebastian said confidently. "Either in the car, or standing at the Memorial. Actually, it doesn't make too much difference whether you get him in the car or standing at the ceremony. So long as you get him. Any questions?"

Nacio's hands stroked his thighs beneath the blanket as he considered the facts given him. Now that the intimate details of the assassination were being examined, he seemed to be oddly relaxed and less tense, more in his element. "Yes, quite a few. For example, what do I do for the week between now and next Tuesday? Sit in the hotel room?"

Sebastian shook his head. "You do not. You use the hotel room—you and Iracema, together or alone—as any other visiting couple would do. You show signs of normal occupancy. You leave toothpaste stains in the washbowl and used razor blades lying around." His voice listed these items with almost mechanical precision; it was obvious he had considered each facet of the problem carefully. "You leave pajamas on the bed, and you drop socks on the floor for the maid to pick up. Iracema leaves tissues around with lipstick stains—things like that." He leaned forward. "And you leave the room each morning at eight o'clock, before the floor maids start on the rooms, and you come back in the evening after dinner, after the floor staff has left for the day. In other words, you do nothing to cause the slightest attention to be drawn to you, but still nothing to make it appear you are avoiding attention. Is that clear?"

Nacio nodded, absorbing the details of the scheme. Sebastian continued his litany.

"And you leave no fingerprints—"

Nacio frowned. "How do you live in a hotel for a week and leave no fingerprints?"

"By wearing gloves. Surgical gloves. I have two pairs for you here. You put them on as soon as you enter the room each night, and you take them off as you leave in the morning. And you remember to wipe the knob of the door each time you use it." He smiled, pleased with himself. "I told you this job was thoroughly planned."

"So it's planned. And all right, I wear the gloves. I don't know how, but I do. What do I do with my time in the hotel room every night?"

"Whatever you want to do, but very little drinking. As a matter of fact, until this job is over, no drinking at all would be better." He shrugged. "You watch television, as most people do. Or you read, or listen to the radio. Or play cards with Iracema—"

Nacio could not prevent the sarcasm. "With gloves on?"

"It'll keep you from cheating," Sebastian said dryly. With Nacio firmly fixed into the scheme, he felt more relaxed, more sure of himself. And, of course, far less afraid of the other. "Any other questions?"

"What do I do during the days? Come here?"

"You do not. You take a taxi away from the center of town each morning; one day to the beach at Copacabana —or Leblon would be even better, it's less crowded. Another day to the Botanical Gardens, or the Zoo—" He shrugged. "We'll lay out a schedule."

"Fine." The smaller man eyed him coldly. "When you're laying it out, though, just remember that every policeman in Rio knows my face."

"Except that you are not going to look like you," Sebastian said calmly. "You will look like Doctor Carabello of Três Rios, who is a man with a full mustache that I have ready for you, and who is a bit older than you and a bit taller than you—or at least who stands straighter than you—and with a full face that some cheek-pads will provide."

Nacio shook his head with exaggerated admiration. "You really did plan this thing, didn't you? About the only thing you've left out is a pair of dark sunglasses . . ."

The sarcasm was disregarded by the heavyset man. "You will definitely *not* wear dark glasses. You're supposed to be a visiting doctor from the interior, not an American tourist. You will wear glasses with thin gold frames and just plain glass in them. You will look quite distinguished, as a matter of fact—the type no policeman would consider twice. Is that clear?"

"If you say so. And does Iracema, my devoted wife, go with me every day? To the beach, I mean, or to the Zoo?"

"No." Sebastian shook his head and smiled faintly. "How many men take their wives to the beach, or anywhere else, in Rio?" His smile faded as an additional precaution occurred to him. "Nor will you take anyone else, or look up any of your old friends, male or female. There'll be plenty of time for that when the job is over. And plenty of money, too, as far as that is concerned."

"Ah, yes." Nacio nodded almost lazily. "Speaking of money, I assume I get an advance? And a sizable one, considering the ultimate fee?" His tone was light, almost bored, but Sebastian recognized the steel in the other's voice.

"One thousand conto."

"Five thousand conto," Nacio corrected, and passed unhurriedly to the next subject. "And the gun?"

For a moment Sebastian looked as if he might argue the question of money, but he changed his mind. It wasn't his money and there was plenty of it. "The gun was stolen over a month ago from the home of a British Embassy employee. It's a good hunting rifle—he must have thought we have elephants here in Brazil—and it can't be traced to us in any way. Iracema will bring it to the hotel the night before the parade. There's no point in having it lying around for a week where some nosy maid or somebody might bump into it."

"I'll need a chance to test it and see if it pulls, and how the sight works."

"When we're through here, you can see it. It's upstairs." Sebastian tilted his head toward the windows, still streaked from the driving rain. "And when it stops raining you can check it all you want outside. Up on that spur it's just woods, and anyway, people around here mind their own business."

"Good enough. And how about a handgun, too?"

Sebastian shook his head. "No handgun."

"You mean you expect me to go around this town for a week with no protection?"

"No handgun." The heavy man's voice was firm. "We're not taking any chances of your getting involved in any arguments. That's definite."

For a few seconds their glances locked; Nacio was the first to look away. "One last thing, then. Will Iracema be with me there—in the room—when I—?"

"No." Sebastian relaxed a bit. "And that's another reason she's in on this plan. She can go where she wants without any suspicion. On the morning of the parade, Iracema will be at the Gloria Hotel and watch the motorcade start. Once it's formed and leaves, she'll telephone you. She'll tell you in which car your man is, and if there's more than one man in the car, which one he is." His eyes were steady on the other. "After that, it's up to you."

"Good enough. And what then? How do I get away after it's over?"

"Afterwards, you'll get away as quickly as possible. While you're doing the job you'll have your television on loud; any program with talking, but no music. Preferably a play or an old movie, but any talking will do. If anyone hears the shot, they'll assume it was part of the program. I know you don't want to use a silencer—"

"Not at that distance."

"Then afterwards, you simply turn the set down and leave the room. You'll also leave all your luggage, none of which will be identifiable. And since the gun can't be traced to anyone except that idiot at the British Embassy, you'll leave that, too. It won't take the police long to find out from which room the shot was fired, in any event. So just shove it out of sight somewhere, and leave."

"And where do I go?"

"You come here. You'll have plenty of time to get clear of the hotel and the area before the excitement strikes there. Just the same, be damned sure you're not followed by anyone. I'll be here, even if Iracema hasn't gotten back yet. After that—" He shrugged. "You take your share and you go."

Nacio pursed his thin lips and considered everything he had heard. It looked possible, as most of Sebastian's schemes were possible, but it also looked a lot more complex than he liked. In most of his previous jobs he had simply walked up to his victim in a bar or on the street, shot him, and then walked away. He appreciated that this case was considerably different, and that obviously very big people were involved to attempt an assassination of this character, but still . . .

Sebastian was becoming impatient. "Well?"

Nacio looked at him coolly. "Well, if you want my opinion, the whole thing is unnecessarily complicated. If you'd simply tell me who you want shot, and then leave the thing to me—"

"No. Not this time. This time we do it just as I've outlined it. Because this time it's essential that you don't get caught and talk." He seemed to realize that his words implied that at previous times it had been less essential; he spread his hands apologetically. "You know what I mean. The people involved in this are paying this fantastic sum to be damned sure they do not become connected with it in any way, and the best assurance of that is for you not to be caught. And the best way not to be caught is to follow the scheme. If you have any changes or improvements, I'm more than willing to listen to them. But the basic scheme stands. Well?"

"Well, I suppose the thing could work . . ."

"Good." Sebastian took this as acceptance and came to his feet. "Then if you'd like to get cleaned up and dressed, the bathroom and your clothes are upstairs. I'll help you with the mustache and the cheek-pads and the rest of your gear. Then you can play with the gun until you're satisfied with it. And tonight we'll go over the whole thing again— or again and again if necessary—until we all have clearly in mind just what you're supposed to do."

"Fair enough." Nacio came out of his chair, drawing the blanket about his lean body. He looked over at the girl, running his eyes slowly and almost insultingly over her charms. "You haven't said much."

Only the faintest heightening of her color indicated her resentment of his inspection. She smiled at him in a disdainful manner. "I only talk when I have something to say."

Nacio studied her a moment more. "I'll appreciate that in the hotel," he said abruptly, and started for the stairs. Suddenly he paused, frowning, looking back over his shoulder at Sebastian.

"Just one last question. You talk about what each one of us is to do to earn this big money. Iracema will be at the Gloria, spotting the man for me. I'll be at the Serrador doing the job. Just what will you be doing?"

The heavyset man smiled; for the first time it seemed to be a genuine smile. The fingers of one fleshy hand rubbed themselves together in a standard Brazilian gesture.

"Me?" he said. "I'll be doing the most important part of the entire job. I'll be arranging to get paid for it. . . ."

Four

THE STORM, with brief interludes, racked the area for another three days and then—apparently deciding it had scrubbed Rio's craggy face enough and that the spectacular city was now presentable for her auspicious Inter-American visitors—abruptly moved off to the north to attempt the same tactics with Belo Horizonte. Its place was immediately taken by a battery of street cleaners, who fought the debris of mud, broken orange crates, and discarded construction lumber that had washed down from the *favelas* above and lodged against the seawalls, covering the patterned mosaic sidewalks of most low-lying streets. True, the street cleaners concentrated their efforts entirely on that portion of the city which the O.A.S. delegates were most likely to visit, but only because this was the most logical thing to do. After all, why accustom the *Carioca* to clean boulevards and debris-free avenues when he would only litter them again in a short time? Besides, under that burning tropical sun the mud would soon be transposed to dust and presumably blown away; and the orange crates and lumber would be snatched back by the slum-dwellers long before the attendants of the cleaning trucks could arrive to commandeer those valuable items for themselves.

Mr. Wilson, driving home that Friday evening from the American Embassy after a particularly frustrating and unproductive day, came through the tunnel that led from Botofogo into Copacabana, swung from the Avenida Princesa Isabel into the Avenida Atlântica, and then hastily braked to avoid running into the bottleneck of traffic that stretched ahead of him as far as he could see. He shifted to neutral to preserve the worn transmission of his five-year-old car, and swayed in jerky rhythm with his asthmatic motor, trying to let the soft evening breeze and the always pleasant sight of the sea pulsing under the full tropical moon wash away the aggravations he had been forced to suffer that day.

To begin with, a stenotypist brought down early from Washington to ensure accurate and unbiased transcriptions of the forthcoming O.A.S. conferences, had occupied two hours of his afternoon by tearfully insisting that she had been pinched on the street by—of all things—a native! It had taken Wilson the greater portion of this wasted time trying to understand why anyone would want to so flatter the woman, and the balance to assure her with a straight face that it undoubtedly was part of a sinister campaign aimed at rattling the nerves of stateside stenotypists, and that she could best serve the interests of her country by pretending to overlook the incident. And she had been followed by a rotund businessman from Zenia, Ohio, who had maintained a bit angrily that when any hostelry of the advertised eminence of the Hotel Miracopa failed to provide water for a guest of his importance, it could only be because they wished to insult citizens of the United States, and just exactly what was the Security Officer going to do about it?

The line of traffic on the Avenida Atlântica edged forward a bit and then, startled by its own temerity, instantly subsided again. Wilson braked automatically, sighed, and from force of habit raised his eyes to the window of an apartment building on the further corner of the next block. To his surprise a light shone at the familiar upper-floor window, which suggested to him that either his rather explosive friend Captain Da Silva was unaccountably at home, or that the apartment was being ransacked by some exceptionally careless thieves. On the slim chance that the former situation obtained, he angled for the curb in search of a parking place. He had nothing planned for the evening and possibly he could have dinner with his old friend. Or even if Da Silva were busy, a drink would still ease some of the tensions of the day and pass time until traffic subsided.

He managed a location between a no-parking sign and a fire hydrant, locked the car, crossed the wide sidewalk and tramped up the five steps that led to the building lobby. The automatic elevator carried him jerkily to the proper floor; he walked down the tiled corridor and leaned on the bell. There was a long wait, sufficient to make him wonder if, perhaps, his second premise might not have been the correct one, and then at last the door swung back. Da Silva, draped in a towel and dripping freely, stared at him a moment and then stood aside, gesturing his welcome with a tilt of his head.

"Hi. Come on in." He stepped back, dragging the towel about himself a bit more securely. "You caught me in the shower. Have a drink while I get dressed." He moved toward an inner door. "I just came home for a breather. I have to get back downtown again."

Wilson nodded, wandered over to the bar, brought forth a bottle and two glasses, and proceeded to fill them generously. He raised his voice to carry into the next room. "Too bad; I was hoping we could eat together." His tone became curious. "Exactly how many hours are you working these days, Zé?"

Da Silva answered from the bedroom. "These days? Twenty-six. Or maybe twenty-eight and they go so fast they only seem like twenty-six. It could also be thirty—I never was very good at arithmetic." He came back into the room in his shorts, carrying trousers and a shirt, and pulled them on. A wall mirror allowed him to comb his thick curly hair into a relative semblance of order. He padded to the bar, still barefooted, and accepted the glass Wilson had provided for him. He winked at the nondescript man in a congenial manner, raised the glass in a small gesture of appreciation, and then drank. He put down his glass, smiling gratefully.

"That's better. I've been so busy the last few days I haven't even had time for my normal drinking. Or even for my abnormal drinking. It's a good thing you came along to handle the bar chores."

"Any time," Wilson said magnanimously. He carried his glass to the coffee table and dropped into a low chair while Da Silva returned to the bedroom for his shoes and socks. The barefooted man came back, retrieved his glass from the bar, and then sat down opposite Wilson to finish dressing. Wilson took a small sip of his drink and studied his friend with a faint smile.

"Why the long hours, Zé? It's quite un-Brazilian, you realize. You might start a trend that could cause you to become the most hated man in the country, if it were ever traced to you, that is." Another possibility seemed to strike him. "Or is it simply that you've become curious as to how we working folks live?"

Da Silva looked up, affronted. His heavy black eyebrows rose dramatically. "This from an officer of the American Embassy? Whose hours begin at noon and end at one P.M., during which time they are permitted to go out for lunch? And are given PX privileges as a reward for this extraordinary devotion to duty? Please!"

"I'm serious." Wilson's smile faded. "Why do you have to go back to work tonight? You look worn out."

"Don't let it fool you," Da Silva said, and grinned. "It's only a disguise. Behind this façade of weariness lies utter exhaustion." His grin was interrupted by a sudden and deep yawn. He shook his head. "I guess I'm so tired I don't even make good nonsense."

Wilson studied him. "So why go back? Is there anything special on the fire?"

Da Silva looked at him a moment curiously, and then shook his head. "Nothing special. It's just that the O.A.S. meeting will start before we know it, and we still have a lot of checking to do."

"And they couldn't do it without you?"

"Let's say I'd hate to think so. I'm too old to look for another job." Da Silva bent forward, studying his large shoes, wondering what there was about them that bothered him. The solution came to him; he leaned over, completed tying the laces, and then fell back again in his chair. "There's still a lot to do. We heard today that our mutual friend Juan Dorcas will be arriving with his retinue in a few days; he's been out of Argentina for the past month or two on a vacation or something, but he's expected back, and he'll be here, so naturally—"

"Traveling? Where?"

Da Silva stared at him sardonically. "Why don't you ask that question of your head office? I'm quite sure you've had a man on his tail ever since he left."

"And I'm quite sure we haven't." Wilson shook his head hopelessly. "You're really stubborn. And still looking under the rug for some of our big, bad C.I.A. agents. . . ."

Da Silva grinned. "If you're an example, I don't suppose they have to be particularly big. And as far as being bad is concerned, I'm sure they're all very sweet to their mothers." His grin faded abruptly. "In any event, Dorcas will be here in a few days, and I want to be sure that no misguided patriot—of any country, including you-know-who—decides to violate our hospitality by doing anything foolish."

Wilson sighed. It was obvious that nothing he could say could convince Da Silva he was wrong. "And how's it been going so far?"

Da Silva shrugged. He reached into the inlaid box on the table, extracted a cigarette, and lit it, shaking the match out almost absentmindedly. "Oh, we've picked up a few people I'm glad will be behind bars during the meetings. If for no other reason than that I won't have to worry about them. And, of course, we also have a fair bag of known pickpockets down at the *Delegacia*." He paused a moment, thinking about his last statement, and then grinned widely. "Which is a bit foolish on our part, when you stop to think about it."

"Foolish?"

"Certainly." Da Silva sat up a bit, his normal puckish humor returning. "With all the foreign visitors we're going to have in Rio in the next week, these light-fingered boys we've got locked up could be bringing in some of that foreign exchange our country needs so desperately. And just think"—he brought one strong finger up abruptly for emphasis—"if they held these meetings in a different country each year, and if the local pickpockets were given proper latitude and even encouragement, in a short time the entire problem of foreign exchange for all of Latin America might be solved."

"But that would mean having more meetings," Wilson objected. "I thought the other day we'd decided on doing away with meetings and using closed television instead."

"Only after our budgets are balanced," Da Silva said. "Once that's accomplished we could do away with these O.A.S. meetings altogether."

"You know, that's really not a bad idea at all," Wilson said approvingly. He pretended to think about it. "We could disband the diplomatic corps completely, and replace them all with skilled pickpockets—"

Da Silva's bushy eyebrows shot up in shock. "What do you mean 'we,' American? Whose pockets do you think are going to have to be picked if this idea of mine is going to work?" He started to smile but ended up with a cavernous yawn instead.

Wilson's lighthearted manner disappeared. "Really, Zé; how important is this checkup tonight? You're beat. You need rest."

"How important?" Da Silva crushed out his cigarette and remained staring at the ashtray as if seeking some answer there. His eyes came up, studying Wilson. "You never know if you don't do it. But this much I'll say—for the information of any interested parties—we're going all out on this, and anyone with any odd ideas would be well advised to reconsider them. Because we're checking out every building between the Hotel Gloria and the *Municipal*, and we also intend to hit every hotel and any other potential trouble spot." He shook his head. "It's amazing how many alleys and windows and doorways and rooftops there are in a city this size. You don't really give it much thought until you have the job of making sure none of them are dangerous."

Wilson was regarding him stonily. "I assume you consider you've given me a message?"

Da Silva looked surprised. "You? As a matter of fact, I've thought for a long time that this apartment might be bugged; my message was for anyone who might be listening."

He pulled himself to his feet and reached for his jacket, hanging from the back of a chair. He shrugged himself into it, waited until Wilson was ready, and walked with him to the door.

"All right," Wilson said quietly. "There's no sense arguing with you. But you'd be ahead of the game by getting some sleep tonight, instead."

"Sleep?" Da Silva looked at him curiously. "When I get tired I'm afraid my English suffers. What is this word 'sleep'?"

"It's what I'm going home to get plenty of," Wilson said. "It's also the excuse for saying my prayers first, which will give me a chance to pray that you come to your senses about the C.I.A. And also," he added, considering, "a chance to pray that I don't have another day like I had today." He considered his companion critically. "It's also something you need badly."

Da Silva reached for the doorknob. "What I badly need," he said seriously, "is for these meetings to end and for all of the delegates to go back home. Preferably in one piece. . . ."

Whatever prayers Wilson offered, or to Whomever he offered them, it was apparent the following Monday morning that at least a portion of them had not been answered. The small businessman from Zenia, Ohio, was back in his office at the American Embassy at nine o'clock sharp, and the patient Security Officer was doing his best to demonstrate interest in his visitor's latest complaint.

It appeared that the Hotel Miracopa not only insulted its American guests by failing to provide water for their necessities, but it went much further. Either the telephone operators did not speak English, which was surely a studied slight to the many Americans staying there; or else (as the rotund man from Zenia truly suspected) they actually *did* speak English but pretended not to, which certainly posed an even more suspicious circumstance. Lost in the limbo of this Laocoönian logic, Mr. Wilson could only manage to nod in an interested manner at regular intervals, and wonder if his entire day was going to be decimated in this same pointless fashion. One good thing, of course, was that no native had pinched the small man from Zenia.

The telephone at his elbow suddenly rang, temporarily saving him from the inevitable question as to what was he going to do about it. Wilson picked the instrument from its cradle, doing his best to appear casual, and not like a drowning man reaching for a drifting life-raft. He shrugged his apologies for the interruption, cutting off the high nasal voice, and turned his attention to the telephone.

"Hello? Yes?"

His secretary answered from her desk in the outer office. "Hi, boss. Do you want to be saved?"

"Profoundly," Wilson said, and thanked the Lord he had been smart enough to pick Mary as a secretary over those more shapely—and even more secretarially talented—applicants.

"Then you're in. It's Dona Ilesia from the Stranger's

Hospital. Crisis number one for the day has just struck.
She wonders if you might be free to discuss it with her."

"Free," Wilson said wholeheartedly, "and deeply grateful. Put her on."

He cupped the receiver and smiled in a pained fashion
at his guest. "I'm sorry, but this shouldn't take too long."

The businessman subsided grumpily, resisting with effort the temptation of speaking his mind. Cavalier treat-
ment, it seemed, was not limited to the local hotels. After
all, if an American citizen couldn't receive priority at his
own embassy, it clearly seemed to be a situation about
which something should be done.

There was a loud click as the call was transferred
through the switchboard; the hospital supervisor's voice
came on the line. She sounded a bit nervous. *"Senhor
Wilson?"*

"Falando. Que posso fazer p'ra Senhora?"

His visitor's eyebrows shot up in evident alarm; he
seemed to find it highly irregular—if not actually sub-
versive—to have an American official speak in a foreign
language, especially in the haloed precincts of the Embassy
itself. Somebody, his glare said, was certainly going to hear
about this! Wilson, reading the other's mind, felt a twinge
of pity for the Ambassador, and bit back a smile.

At the other end of the line, Dona Ilesia hesitated un-
certainly; when she finally spoke, her voice was troubled.
"I dislike bothering you, Senhor Wilson, but I honestly
don't know what to do. The Air Force has been through
to me twice this morning, once when I first came in and
again just a few minutes ago. About this sailor—"

Wilson frowned at the telephone, his good spirits wan-
ing. Had he been interrupted in the middle of one idiotic
conversation only to fall into another? It would be quite
unusual, since Dona Ilesia was normally the most level-

headed of women, but on a day like today, anything was possible.

"The Air Force? About a sailor?" He stared at the instrument in his hand with a puzzled expression. "What does the Air Force have to do with sailors?" His tone implied that he would also like to know what the whole thing, or even any part of it, had to do with him.

"You don't understand, Senhor Wilson." Dona Ilesia took a deep breath and tried again. "The captain of this ship, this freighter *Santa Eugenia,* has cabled them from Montevideo asking how his steward is getting along. And naturally they called me. Twice. And I don't know what to tell them."

Wilson shook his head as if to clear it of fog, or the effects of too much liquor. "And you're quite right, Dona Ilesia—"

"Quite right? About what, Senhor Wilson?"

"About my not understanding." He clenched the receiver tightly, trying to make some sense of her words. "Since the hospital is involved somehow, the only thing I can imagine is that this sailor you're talking about was, or is, a patient. I still don't see where the Air Force comes into it, or why the captain of this freighter didn't cable the hospital directly to find out about his man—"

"Because he wouldn't know which hospital had him. I mean, which hospital the Sea Rescue Squad would send the man to, once they got him to land. After all, there are over twenty hospitals in Rio. They might have sent him to—"

"Ah!" Wilson drew a deep breath and smiled as the pieces of the mystery began to fall into place. He felt justifiably proud of having managed to make sense from the garbled clues he had been furnished. "Now I think I see what happened. You're saying the Sea Rescue Squad took a sick sailor from this ship and then sent him to us; or rather, to you. And now his captain has arrived at his next port, and being the humanitarian he is, wants to know how he's getting along. Actually," he added, thinking about it, "not an unreasonable request. So what's the problem?"

"But—"

"Ah!" Wilson said, going further in his analysis. "You're worried about security, and whether it's involved. What nationality was this ship?"

"Portuguese, but—"

"Portuguese, eh? Not Russian, eh? Well, in that case tell them what they want to know."

"But I can't tell them!" Dona Ilesia was almost wailing. "You still don't understand, Senhor Wilson! He never got to the hospital. He's the one that disappeared from our ambulance." Her voice changed subtly, becoming slightly accusing, as if in this manner to somehow share the blame. "You should remember, Senhor Wilson. You were there when I came into the Trustees' meeting and told you all about it."

"Oh? Ah! So that's the one, eh? I see. . . ." At long last the thing made sense. Why hadn't the woman given him all the facts in the first place? He thought about the problem a moment and then nodded. "Well, I can see your problem. It's a bit embarrassing, of course, but I suppose we can't exactly keep it a secret. At any rate, no longer. Well, we'll simply have to tell them the man never got to the hospital. I don't see how they can hold us accountable in any way; he obviously got out of the ambulance of his own volition. So tell them . . ." He paused, frowning at his desk, trying to frame a possible answer in properly diplomatic language.

"Tell them what, Senhor Wilson?"

"I'm thinking. Let me see . . . Tell them that this sailor—"

The expression on his face suddenly froze as the full import of the supervisor's words came to him. His eyes came up to stare at the wall opposite, without seeing either its poor paint job or the modernistic daub selected by the Ambassador's wife. A sailor? Taken from a ship at sea by the Sea Rescue Squad? Brought to land and placed in an ambulance without the blessings of either the police or Immigration? And then conveniently disappearing from the vehicle?

"Senhor Wilson? Are you there? You were saying?"

He came to life, his mind still racing. One hand tightened convulsively on the telephone receiver while the other reached swiftly for a pencil and then dragged a lined pad into place before him. "Don't tell them a thing!" He realized his voice had risen and forced it lower. "Don't tell them anything. I'll handle the entire matter." He lifted the pencil and lowered his voice even further, trying to sound noncommittal. "Now, who called you from the Air Force?"

"A certain— One moment, please. I have it written down." There was a brief pause. "Here it is. A Major Barbosa, from the Sea Rescue Squad. Their offices are at the military base, across from Galeão Airport. Would you like their telephone number?"

"Please." Wilson scrawled it down and then underlined it sharply. He thought a moment, shook his head, then nodded, and finally returned his attention to the telephone. "And the sailor's name?"

"I'm afraid I don't have it. This Major Barbosa didn't—"

"All right. Don't worry about it; it's not important. What was the name of the ship's captain; the one that called—or cabled, rather? And the name of the ship again?"

Dona Ilesia sounded even more apologetic, particularly in view of Mr. Wilson's readiness to assist. "I'm sorry, but I don't have the captain's name either. But"—her voice brightened—"I remember the ship was called the *Santa Eugenia*. They couldn't stop at Rio because of the storm, but now that they've docked at Montevideo, the captain— I wish I could remember his name!—naturally wanted to know—"

"Naturally," Wilson said, cutting smoothly into the flow of words. He stared at his pad, wondering what other information he might elicit, and then decided he had gotten all he could get from the hospital supervisor. "I think that's all I'll need, then. I'll take care of everything. And thank you."

"I owe you the thanks, Senhor Wilson. I really appreciate this." Dona Ilesia's relief was clear in her voice. "I honestly didn't know what to tell this major. As you know, this is the first time in the history of Stranger's Hospital that anything like—"

"I'm sure," Wilson said hastily. "And thank you again."

But Dona Ilesia was not finished. "—this ever happened. I hated to bother you, because I know how busy a man like you must be, especially working at the American Embassy, but I tried to reach Senhor Weldon first, and they told me he was out at Gavea playing golf."

"He usually is," Wilson said idly, and then realized that this was no way to break off a conversation. He cleared his throat authoritatively. "Just don't worry about a thing, Dona Ilesia. That's what trustees are for." And at long last we know what they're for, he said to himself, and placed the receiver firmly back on its cradle.

He swiveled his chair and stared at the wall in deep concentration, reviewing the facts she had given him. A sailor taken by helicopter from a ship in mid-ocean, brought to shore and delivered to an ambulance. . . . The whole thing, of course, might be exactly what it purported to be, a foreign sailor suffering from a bad appendix who panicked at the thought of being operated on in a strange place by strange doctors. On the other hand, there was also the chance that it was not. And in any event, the proper man to get in touch with under the circumstances would be his old friend Captain Zé Da Silva.

He reached for the telephone again and then became aware that he was not alone. The gentleman from Zenia, Ohio, was clearing his throat in a manner that clearly indicated his resentment at being disregarded. Wilson flashed him a rueful smile to calm him, erased it immediately, and lifted the receiver.

"Mary, would you please get Captain Da Silva?"

"You mean that beautiful hunk of man? Get him? I'd love to, boss, but he—"

"On the telephone, Mary! And we can discuss your problems some other time."

"Well, all right. . . ."

He sat waiting impatiently, his fingers drumming restlessly on the desk. The man across from him glowered at this continued rudeness, but Wilson paid him no attention. One smile was enough, especially with a nuisance like this one. At last the instrument gave him the connection he wanted and he took over from his secretary, leaning over his desk and speaking with intensity.

"Zé? This is Wilson. I—"

"Wilson?" At the other end of the line, Da Silva leaned back in his desk chair and smiled genially at the telephone. An assistant, waiting at his side with a pile of reports, was waved to wait. A conversation with his American friend was always relaxing, and after the stack of reports he had gone through that morning, a little relaxation would be welcome. Besides, a conversation with any member of the American Embassy staff at the present might also prove fruitful. "How are you? What's on your mind?"

"It's—" Wilson glanced across his desk and then dropped into Portuguese. "It's something I'd rather not discuss on the telephone. But it might be very important. How about dropping your work awhile and meeting me some place?"

Da Silva glanced at the wall clock in his office, made an addition of ten minutes for its normal error, and frowned. He had always thought the police department had purchased the clock at an auction from an old English pub. "Can it wait until lunch? I think I can break away for awhile around noon. We can meet at Santos Dumont. Same place, same time."

"Unfortunately, the same food." Wilson stared at the instrument. "I'd really like to make it sooner. Or wait! That might be even better. It will give me time to do some checking."

"Checking? On what?"

"On disapproving one of your wild theories about one of the organizations I belong to."

Da Silva grinned at the telephone. "I'm sometimes wild, but my theories never are. Take all the time you want, and I wish you the best of luck. I'll see you at noon."

"All right," Wilson said, "but this time you'll have to break all your rules and be prompt. I think I've run across something that might be very interesting. And very hot."

"Is she anyone I know?"

"I'm serious. Be prompt."

"I'm always prompt." Da Silva considered his words

and then made a concession. "However, today I'll be even prompter. How's that?"

"That's fine. Let's also hope it's true. I'll see you at noon, then. *Ciao.*"

He depressed the button of the telephone in preparation for making another call, and then became aware that his visitor by now was glaring at him in full-blown anger, and even beginning to sputter. Wilson sighed and withdrew his hand from the instrument.

"I'm sorry, Mr.—er—um; I'm sorry, sir, but something quite important has come up. I'm afraid I'm going to be tied up for awhile." A better solution to the problem occurred to him. "Tell me, sir, how much longer do you plan on being in Rio?"

"Only two days more." It was almost a bark.

"Oh? Ah, fine! I mean, we might still be able to find time to discuss the matter. Why not give all the information to my secretary? I'll call her." He clicked the button several times and then spoke into the instrument. A moment later Mary appeared in the doorway, glancing sympathetically at her boss. Wilson rose to his feet.

"Mary, this is Mr.—um—this is a gentleman from Ohio who would like to give you some notes regarding a problem of some sort at the Miracopa Hotel. I wonder if you might—"

"Of course, Mr. Wilson."

"Thank you." Wilson held his hand out to his guest; the businessman from Zenia barely touched it. Wilson smiled. "It's been a great pleasure, sir. Always pleased to be of assistance to a fellow American. What we're here for, actually. I'm sorry we couldn't chat longer."

His visitor merely growled deep in his throat.

"And have a good trip home, sir. Good-bye."

Mary took the small man gently but firmly by the arm and led him from the room. Wilson's forced smile disappeared the minute the door closed on the disgruntled gentleman from Ohio, and he dropped back into his chair, reaching for the telephone again. Good God! What was the man's complaint? That the telephone operators at the Miracopa Hotel didn't speak English? Wilson tried to picture a Brazilian complaining to his consulate in New York that the help at the Statler didn't speak Portuguese, and then wiped the incident from his mind. He clicked the button.

"Mary? Put me on an outside line and tell the operator there will be a series of overseas priority calls. And they have to be completed fast." A faint smile spread across his face. "I have a luncheon date with your dream man, Captain Da Silva, and I'd hate to be late. . . ."

Five

EVEN AT TWELVE-THIRTY, quite early by Brazilian standards, the mezzanine restaurant of the Santos Dumont Airport was beginning to crowd. Wilson pushed his way through the closely set tables, ignoring the combination clatter of silverware, hum of voices, and roar of aircraft that came from the runways beneath the open windows, until he managed to locate Da Silva seated alone near the railing overlooking the main floor of the long, modern building. He swung a chair back from the table and sat down, grinning at his friend. Da Silva merely glared back.

"This is your idea of noon sharp?"

Wilson looked at him innocently. "You mean I'm late?" He shook his head in wonder. "I knew if I stayed around here long enough, some of the national habits would rub off." He looked across the table curiously. "By the way, how does it feel to be on time for a change?"

"Terrible," Da Silva admitted, and found himself smiling despite himself. "I know I wouldn't like it as a steady diet." He turned in his chair, snapping his fingers loudly for a waiter, his smile fading. "We're going to have to make it short today, though. I left my desk piled to the ceiling with work. And I want to get a few more things organized before tonight. I'd also like to get some sleep tonight if I can."

"How are things going, by the way?" Wilson's voice contained only polite interest, but his eyes were extremely steady on his friend's face. "Any incidents over the weekend?"

"No," Da Silva said, "but we really didn't expect any. The period we're most concerned with starts tomorrow with that pointless motorcade, and lasts until these meetings are over. And also the man I'm most worried about, our friend Dorcas, won't arrive until this evening. After which, whether he knows it or not, he's going to be covered like a nut sundae." He thought a moment. "Or whether he likes it or not."

He suddenly realized that no waiter was responding to his finger-snapping and reached out in a predatory manner, grasping a passing waiter by the arm. He ordered their usual cognac and then turned back to Wilson.

"Now, what was on your mind that was so important that you arrived here a half-hour late to tell me?"

Wilson looked across the table a moment and then leaned forward. "Do you remember that character that got lost from one of Stranger's Hospital's ambulances last week?"

Da Silva stared at him. "Who?"

Wilson remained patient. "You must remember. It was about a week ago—the last time we had lunch together. In the middle of that terrible storm, remember?

Our ambulance picked him up and he was gone by the time they got him to the hospital?"

"Oh!" Da Silva nodded, the incident returning to his mind. A faint grin creased his lips. "Now I recall it. He was the advanced appendix case. The one we decided would be suffering from double pneumonia or flat feet when you found him. And also flying. Well, with all those clues you should have found him, and from that glint in your eye I gather you did."

"No," Wilson said quietly, "we didn't find him. We didn't even look for him. But I have a strong feeling that you will. And with all the men you can muster."

"You? Meaning me?"

"You, meaning the entire Brazilian police force, in all its pristine glory."

Da Silva stared at him with slightly narrowed eyes. "Overlooking your obvious ignorance as to what the word 'pristine' means—not to mention 'glory'—just why should the Brazilian police waste time on this obvious nut? And even if we managed to catch him, what crime would we charge him with? Leaving the scene of an ambulance?" The thought seemed to amuse him; he snapped his fingers. "I have a better one. We arrest him for failure to pay his fare on a public vehicle."

"If you're through trying to be cute," Wilson said coldly, "I'll tell you why. Because he happened to be a sailor, and the Air Force people were the ones who delivered him to our ambulance. From Galeão Airport," he added significantly.

Da Silva frowned at him and then looked up as a waiter bent to place a bottle and two tall-stemmed glasses on the table. The swarthy Brazilian acknowledged the service with a thankful nod, and then poured the two glasses full. He started to push one across the table and then hesitated. When he spoke his voice reflected his doubts.

"Wilson, are you sure the reason you were late wasn't because you stopped in a bar some place? You sound as if you may have had a couple too many as it is."

Wilson nodded, not at all perturbed. "Exactly what I thought when Dona Ilesia relayed the information to me." He reached across the table, retrieving his drink, and then bent forward, his voice serious. Da Silva, from long experience with the smaller man, listened carefully. When Wilson assumed this attitude, it was usually wise to pay attention.

"This man," Wilson said quietly, turning his glass between his thin fingers and watching Da Silva's face closely, "was a sailor—a steward—on a freighter called the *Santa Eugenia*. The ship was originally scheduled to dock here in Rio, but because of the storm, and because the ship was in bad balance because of its cargo, the captain decided to pass up both Rio and Santos and go directly to Montevideo." He brought his glass to his lips, sipped, and set it down. "Well, just after the captain came to this decision—and had a notice posted to the effect for the benefit of the crew and the passengers—this steward supposedly became deathly ill. Suddenly and with no previous warning. . . ."

Da Silva was listening closely now. "And?"

"And the captain, afraid of taking any chance that a sailor might die on him, and unable to dock, got in touch with the Sea Rescue Squad here by radio, and they sent out a helicopter and brought the man to shore. They had already called for an ambulance—"

Da Silva's eyebrows had risen. "They brought him ashore in a helicopter in the middle of that storm?"

"That's right."

Da Silva shuddered; it was not acting. "Better him than me! The thought of being in any aircraft, but especially a helicopter in that weather!" He grimaced and then looked up. "I'm sorry. Go ahead."

"Well, that's about it. They picked him up, brought him ashore, and delivered him to the Stranger's Hospital Ambulance at Galeão."

Da Silva stared at him intently a moment and then up-ended his drink. He reached for the bottle. "And from the ambulance he disappeared on the way to the hospital."

"Exactly." Wilson nodded and leaned back. "I thought you might find it interesting."

"Damned interesting." Da Silva stared at the bottle a moment and then slowly refilled his glass. He studied the amber liquid as if trying to see a clear motive in the depths of the cognac. "It would be a rather neat way to get into the country without going through the formality of Customs, or Immigration . . ."

"Or the police, either, if it comes to that," Wilson added.

"Especially when we were checking out all airplanes and ships from top to bottom. It would be a very cute gimmick, indeed. Unless, of course"—Da Silva frowned— "the man really was sick and needed attention."

"You knocked holes in that argument the other day," Wilson objected. "You pointed out that no man who was genuinely sick was going to leave an ambulance, especially in the middle of that storm."

"That's true," Da Silva admitted. "But that was before I knew about his coming ashore by helicopter. It's hard to believe that any man would do that unless he had a desperate reason."

"Exactly," Wilson agreed softly. "But that desperate reason doesn't necessarily have to be a bad appendix. . . ."

"I suppose not." The swarthy face frowned; the black eyes came up. "By the way, where did you get all this information?"

Wilson shrugged. "The captain of the ship cabled the Air Force to find out how the man was, and the Air Force called the hospital. All very *delicado* and routine. And the hospital called me, since they had no idea of how to explain a lost patient, and apparently felt that trustees did. And then once the facts finally clicked in my brain—"

"You checked back."

"Right." Wilson raised his glass, smiled at it, and then drank it. He reached for the bottle. "And found that the ship was still docked in Montevideo, unloading, and its personnel were available for questioning."

"And this questioning was done by whom?"

Wilson looked at him steadily. "By Interpol, if you must know. Not by the C.I.A."

"I see." Da Silva's face was expressionless. "And what was this mysterious steward's name?"

Wilson dug into a pocket and brought out some papers. He leafed through them and finally extracted one. "Here it is. On the ship's manifest he was listed as Cacarico. Z. Cacarico."

"*What!*"

Wilson stared at him. "Do you know him?"

The somber expression changed to a broad, but slightly rueful grin. "Whoever this character is, he either has a sense of humor or he's smart enough to pick a name that probably few Portuguese recall if they ever knew it. For your information, Cacarico was a rhinoceros in the São

Paulo zoo who was elected in a write-in campaign some years ago to the House of Representatives."

Wilson looked interested. "And how did he do?"

"They wouldn't seat him. I forget now if it was because he wouldn't swear allegiance to the flag, or because he couldn't salute it. Or maybe because he might represent too much competition to the other solons."

Wilson shook his head sadly. "Well, that's politics."

Da Silva's smile faded. "Whatever it is, it seems to put the finish on any arguments of mine. Anyone who comes into this country the way this one did, with a name obviously picked from the blue, especially in times such as these, certainly does rate being picked up by the police." He glanced at his watch and started to rise. "And today don't tell me we haven't eaten because I know it. And resent it. But, also knowing the Brazilian police, I think we ought to get them started on the job as soon as possible."

"A fine way to talk about your colleagues," Wilson said chidingly. "Sit down and relax. The plane from Montevideo won't be in for at least another four hours. We'll have lots of time for a good meal—if they've got one here—and you can still spend a few hours at your desk before they arrive."

"Whose plane from Montevideo?"

"Well," Wilson said slowly, "that's a bit hard to say. Officially, of course, it was assigned to the delegates to the conferences beginning tomorrow. Unofficially, I suppose it belongs to the American people. In any event, since no one was using it, I'm afraid I arranged to have it fly down to Montevideo. A blow to the crew, since they probably figured they had a week's unearned vacation to investigate the beaches and fleshpots, but that's the way it goes."

"I'm sorry I put it that way." Da Silva sounded anything but sorry. "I meant, what plane?"

"What plane? Why, the one with the pictures, of course," Wilson said cheerfully.

"Pictures?" Da Silva smiled across the table, but it was a taut smile, and there was steel beneath the softness of his voice. "You know, Wilson, I have an odd feeling you're trying to tell me something."

"You noticed that, eh? Well, as usual, you're right. I'm trying to tell you the chances are good that we have some pictures of the man we're talking about."

"Pictures?"

Wilson shrugged. "Photographs, anyway. If you were expecting oils, I'm sorry. But even these are a break, because the descriptions the Interpol man down there got from the crew were about as useful as pockets on a shroud. A composite of what they told him would have resulted in a man anywhere from four to eight feet tall."

"How about fingerprints?"

"After almost a week? Not on that ship. But, as I say, we got a break with the pictures. Or anyway, maybe. The captain was cooperative enough, but he barely remembered they had a steward, let alone what he looked like. To him a steward was just a body in a white jacket; and, of course, a statistic to be checked when it got sick. However—"

"Well, let's hear it!" Da Silva was close to barking. "Don't drag it out into an eight-part serial!"

"*Calma,*" Wilson said evenly, and then grinned. "After all, I did all the work, so let me have the fun of telling it my way." He took a deliberate drink and set his glass down. "As I was saying, it seems the first mate, a promising lad named Miguel, bought himself a fancy Japanese camera in Funchal when they stopped there, and after that he took quite a few candid shots around and about the ship—two rolls, as a matter of fact. He thinks—mind you, he doesn't know for sure—but he thinks our elusive steward may have unconsciously figured in some of them."

"He thinks? Why doesn't he simply look at the pictures?"

"I can tell you're upset," Wilson said. "Not thinking clearly. Obviously because they haven't been developed yet. The ship hasn't been in any one port long enough to get them back from a processor. He was planning on having them done in Buenos Aires."

"I see," Da Silva said slowly. "Instead of which we'll develop them for him—free of charge—in our police laboratory here."

"Right!" Wilson said, and smiled at him proudly. The character of his smile changed slightly. "Actually, I didn't know it would be free of charge, but I think it's a nice gesture."

Da Silva considered him seriously. "Just one question," he said slowly. "Granting you used your head this morning, and did a nice bit of follow-up, just how do you expect this to clear your C.I.A. of my nasty accusations?"

"Well," Wilson said a bit expansively, "if this suspicious steward is uncovered through my efforts—and I have faith in you to do it—and if he should prove to be one of the bad guys, and if all this walking hand-in-hand into the sunset comes about through my modest efforts, then"—he raised his shoulders, but the light tone of his voice had somehow diminished—"then, obviously, it has to clear the C.I.A. of any suspicion, at least in connection with him. Because otherwise why would I do it?" He became completely serious. "Look, Zé; I don't deny that there might be a try at Dorcas. There has been in the past. But if there is, we have nothing to do with it. I want that understood. And that's why I've been breaking my back try-

ing to dig up anything that might identify, and at least—
well, say disarm—any potential assassin."

Da Silva looked at him wonderingly.

"You are marvelous!" he said with admiration. "You
are absolutely incredible. Fantastic! I love the way that
brain of yours works. I especially love the way you assume
I never heard of the word 'decoy' or any of its thesaurian
synonyms." He leaned forward. "I'm not saying I don't
want to see these photographs of yours, because I do. What
I'm saying, simply, is this: if the United States feels it imperative to uplift us poor ignorant heathens, why do they
insist on sending us such unimpressive things as money?
Or wide-eyed youngsters to build us ice hockey rinks in
the middle of the Amazon jungle? Why don't they simply
send us more Wilsons?"

Wilson considered him with a jaw that was tightening
perilously. For several moments there was a charged silence at the table. Then Wilson took a deep breath and
forced himself to smile.

"More Wilsons?" he asked, and then shook his head.
"Why? You don't know what to do with the ones you already have. . . ."

He turned abruptly and raised his arm for the waiter.

The late afternoon sun, flooding Da Silva's fifth-floor
office in the old Instituto de Estudios Academicos, slanted
insidiously through the Venetian blinds and threw bars
of shadow across the city map that covered one full wall
of the room. Under the blaze of light the various colored
pins all assumed the same shade of burnished gold, losing
identity. Da Silva walked over, drew the blinds, and then
walked back to his post beside the map. The two detectives waiting for him watched their boss stolidly.

At one side Wilson sat quietly, watching the repeat of a

performance he had witnessed since dropping off the negatives some half-hour before. Some long hours of subjective thought had removed most of the anger he had felt at lunch; under similar conditions he knew he would have acted much as Da Silva was acting. And watching Da Silva delegate the various jobs and cover the possible trouble sources, he wondered if he would act as efficiently.

Da Silva's finger reached toward the map and then retracted. He smiled wearily.

"You don't need a map to know where the Hotel Serrador is. At any rate, that's your assignment for tonight. Every room, but first and principally, the rooms that face the bay. And the ones on the upper floors—above the fourth. If you have time, the rest of the rooms as well, but first those. I want to know—" He shook his head apologetically. "I'm sorry. I've gone through this often enough with you before. You both know what we're looking for."

Sergeant Ramos nodded slowly. He was a man as large as Da Silva, with even wider shoulders; his almost Indian features showed no emotion. His jaws chewed steadily on a wad of gum; his large hands were jammed into his pockets. His companion, equally large and tough-looking, stood back a step and waited.

"All right," Da Silva said. "Get something to eat and then get to it."

Sergeant Ramos paused in his gum chewing and cleared his throat. "It's going to take quite a while, Captain. How late do we work?"

Da Silva's eyebrows went up dangerously. Sergeant Ramos hastened to clarify his question. "I don't mean that, Captain. I mean, how late are we supposed to disturb people?"

"Oh." Da Silva frowned at the floor for several moments. "Midnight, I suppose. Of course some of the guests won't even be in by then, and you'll probably wake some others, but that's unfortunate. Try to cover as many as you can, and be as diplomatic as possible. But check them out just the same. All right?"

"Right, sir."

Ramos marched from the room, followed quietly by his partner a step behind. Da Silva walked over and dropped into the swivel chair back of his paper-strewn desk. He rubbed the back of his neck a few moments to relieve the tension, and then leaned over and pressed a button on his desk. The door popped open immediately; his young aide, Ruy, stood rigidly in the doorway.

"Captain?"

"Those two rolls of pictures Senhor Wilson gave you," Da Silva said evenly. "They've been in the lab for over half an hour now. What the devil are they doing with them? Tinting them for Christmas presents?"

"They said they'd let me know—"

"The devil with what they said! Go down there and stand on their backs until they're ready!"

"Yes, sir!"

The door closed smartly behind the young man. Wilson came to his feet, walking over to stand beside the desk, speaking sympathetically. "Take it easy, Zé. Relax."

"Relax? I'll relax when this business is over." The tall, swarthy Brazilian leaned back in his chair, thinking. "You know, I think when this next week is over, I really will relax. I think I'll take a week off and go up to the *fazenda*. Do some hunting and fishing. Get some decent rest." He smiled up at the man at his side. "How about taking some of your vacation and joining me?"

"Me?" Wilson grinned at him. "You may have me behind bars by then, remember?"

"True." Da Silva appeared to think about it. "Well, for that week I'll arrange a parole for you."

"In that case I'll be happy to."

"Good. We'll—"

The door opened to admit Ruy; the young man crossed the room and handed an envelope to Da Silva. The tall detective sat straighter in his chair, reaching over to flip the button on his desk lamp. He tipped up the envelope, took the two small packs of photographs that slid out, and started going through the first pack. Wilson bent over while Ruy looked down over his superior's other shoulder.

Da Silva glanced at the first, slid it behind the others, and looked at the second. He grunted. "He may have a good camera, but you'd never know it from these pictures."

"That's what the lab said took so long, Captain," Ruy explained. "The pictures on that roll were all overexposed. The lab said it was common on board ship with amateurs."

Da Silva looked up at Wilson sardonically. "So do me a great favor the next time you dig up a deal like this. Make sure your photographer is a bit more professional."

"Consider it done," Wilson said, and watched as Da Silva returned his attention to the stack of photographs. He flipped aside those that merely showed bits of the ship and a few that failed to show even this much, and then paused as he came to one that had more detail. A faint frown crossed his face; he reached into a drawer and brought out a magnifying glass, bringing it closer to the picture. Wilson leaned farther forward. As far as he could see it only showed the back of a man leaning over the rail of the ship; the small amount of profile scarcely served for identification. In the background a hazy sea extended to fill the frame.

"What is it, Zé?"

Da Silva studied the picture for several moments with narrowed eyes, and then shook his head slowly. "Nothing. For a moment I thought . . ." He shrugged and slid the picture under the pile, continuing to study the others one at a time. The first photograph came back to view; he tossed the pack aside and reached for the second packet.

"Ah. This is better. Apparently when he came to his second roll of film he decided to read the book first."

The pictures in the second roll had improved greatly in quality, if not in subject matter. Poorly framed shots of the deck and some of the cargo still showed too much sky and sea; the composition was amateurish, but at least the pictures themselves were sharp and clear. Da Silva went through them one at a time, slowly studying each one before sliding it to the rear of the pack. At his side Wilson began to fear his efforts had been wasted.

Then suddenly Da Silva's fingers tightened on a newly exposed photograph; he leaned forward, his eyes alive. Ruy, bending over his shoulder, let out a gasp. Wilson leaned over.

"Who is he, Zé?"

Da Silva drew the picture closer, but there was no doubt at all in his mind. The small photograph showed a man in a white steward's jacket dumping a pail of garbage over the taffrail. Sea gulls poised behind the ship, frozen in the air; the curling wake was clearly discernible. The man's face was turned three-quarters toward the camera, but it was obvious he was unaware of being photographed. The high widow's peak, the sharp nose, the thin lips, were instantly identifiable.

Da Silva looked up at Ruy, his eyes sharp, his voice conveying his urgency. "His dossier!"

"Yes, sir!" Ruy disappeared from the room. Wilson stared down at the photograph and then at Da Silva's intent expression.

"Who is he, Zé?"

Da Silva stared at the picture, his eyes narrowed, and then looked up. "This is a man named Nacio Madeira Mendes. A professional killer. Who escaped while on his way to prison three years ago." His eyes went back to the picture. His voice was even, but deadly. "So dear Nacio is back with us again. . . ."

Ruy came hurriedly back into the room and laid a folder on Da Silva's desk. The grim-faced detective flipped it open. Clipped to the back of the cover was a pair of large police photographs, front and profile, with fingerprint classifications printed below. He slipped it loose and laid it on his desk, leafed through the sheets in the folder a moment, and then picked out the top two, handing them up to Wilson.

"Read it for yourself. That's his history."

Wilson took the sheets, straightening up to read them. His eyebrows raised. "Twelve known assassinations . . ." He read to the end; the room was silent until he had finished. When he handed the pages back to Da Silva his face was equally grim. "A bad boy, eh?"

"A real bad boy."

"And yet," Wilson said wonderingly, "he's been here a week and nothing has happened yet." He frowned. "Maybe he just decided to come home at this time. It doesn't necessarily mean a connection with the O.A.S. meetings."

"Nacio didn't decide to come home just for fun," Da

Silva said darkly. "He's been holed up somewhere—apparently in Europe, if he came over on a Portuguese freighter —and we had no idea where. And now he chooses this time to come back, and Rio to come back to, where every policeman knows him, and at a time we have an exceptionally active security in operation." He shook his head worriedly. "No. He came here to do a job. And it would have to be a pretty big job; one that would pay enough to make him take the risk."

"Has he ever done any political killing before?"

Da Silva shrugged toward the folder on the desk. "You read the record. Nacio is as apolitical as he is amoral. He couldn't care less. He's strictly a gun for hire. He'd kill his best friend if the price was right."

"And you think he might be here in connection with Dorcas?"

Da Silva studied the map on the wall without seeing it. He swiveled his chair and stared at Wilson. "What I think is that he came here to do a killing. It might be Dorcas, or it might be someone else. The fact that he hasn't killed anyone up to now—or at least that we know of— only leads me to believe even more that it's in connection with the O.A.S. meetings, because most of those people are only now arriving." He shook his head bitterly. "We're really going to have to tighten up on security, and God knows how we can tighten up any more. Or where we'll get the men. Or even what use it will be, especially against a professional like Nacio Mendes!"

"It could still be a private affair," Wilson said slowly. "After all, someone must have hired him, and if I were a middleman arranging an assassination, I'd pick someone whose face isn't as well known as you say this Nacio's is."

"And if I were a middleman hiring him, I'd get him to change his appearance." Da Silva nodded thoughtfully. "And that's an idea. . . . Ruy, get Jaime in here." He looked up at Wilson. "Jaime is one of our police artists. And damned good. Let's see what he can do for us."

He leaned back, his eyes staring broodingly toward the darkened windows. "Somewhere in this town, Nacio Madeira Mendes is loose. The thought of trouble before was bad enough, but now it's absolutely frightening."

"How about his known haunts? I see the dossier says something about his having a piece of the Maloca de Tijuca." His face reddened slightly. "I happen to know the place. . . ."

A faint smile appeared on Da Silva's face. "You should be ashamed of yourself! It's not the most reputable bar out on the beach. And the girls in back are certainly not the finest Rio has to offer." His smile disappeared. "In any event, he sold his interest a year before we caught up with him. And besides, I doubt that he'd take any chance of showing up at a familiar place, not if the job he came to do is as big as I think it is. And of course," he added bitterly, "we don't have the men available to check the place out anyway."

"I still think it might be worth it," Wilson said stubbornly. "He had to go somewhere to get a weapon; I'm sure he wasn't figuring on strangling his victim. He's always used a gun. And he certainly didn't bring one with him all the way from Lisbon. Or from the ship."

"Which only means the thing was set up well ahead of time. Which makes the whole thing even more frightening."

"How about his family? Or friends? Or known associates?"

Da Silva shook his head. "Nothing. I know, professional killers work through agents, middlemen who hire them and pay them off, but we've never been able to find out who hired him in the past. And we tried when we had him. He's a tough little monkey. We—"

He broke off as the door opened. Ruy ushered in a tall thin man with a shock of white hair and sharp blue eyes, who carried a large tablet of paper under one arm. The newcomer nodded politely to the men in the room and seated himself comfortably at a chair beside the desk. One thin hand reached out and picked up the small photograph of the steward, studying it impartially. He compared it to the police photograph and then nodded.

"He's lost weight. . . ."

He seemed to be talking to himself. He crossed his legs, settling the large pad against one thigh, and then closed his eyes almost to slits, staring at the picture.

Da Silva watched him. "Do you know what we want?" Jaime nodded absently, and then opened his eyes, beginning to sketch rapidly. The first drawing was a duplicate of the three-quarter profile of Nacio as shown in the small photograph. He nodded as he finished it, tore it off and placed it where he could refer to it, and then seemingly repeated it. This time, however, he added a mustache, studied it a moment, and then thickened it a bit. The shape didn't seem to please him and he erased the corners, drawing them down a bit. Then, satisfied at last, he tore this sheet off and repeated the entire performance. The other men in the room watched him in silent admiration.

This time Jaime added eyeglasses, heavy-rimmed, studious frames, with thick bars going back to hook behind the ears. A thin hairline mustache was placed beneath the thin nose, and then broadened a bit. This sketch joined the rest, and he started once again. His thin fingers drew the outline of the familiar face once again with incredible speed and skill and then paused. The blue eyes came up inquiringly.

"What else might he use, Captain?"

Da Silva shrugged. "I have no idea. Put a hat on him. That widow's peak is fairly distinctive."

Jaime nodded in agreement and rapidly sketched in a hat. It was a straw hat, of the type most common in the hot climate. He placed a wide band about the brim and stared at it; on the pad Nacio looked off into the distance, debonair and scholarly. "What else, Captain?"

Da Silva sighed. "God knows. One of these ought to look like him, if he isn't going around in a dress and a wig. We'll have to work with these, I guess." He smiled gratefully. "Thanks, Jaime."

"Any time, Captain." The thin man unfolded himself from the chair, nodded to the others, and left the room, softly closing the door behind him. Da Silva spread the sketches across his desk, studied them a moment, and then brought them together in a small pile.

"Ruy—copies of these at once to all precincts. With the usual information. And rush!"

"Right, Captain." Ruy scooped up the pictures and left.

Wilson frowned. "Sometimes you puzzle me, Zé. Granted the sketches are a good idea, but do you mean you hope to pick him up on the offhand chance that someone from one of your precincts might run into him on the street and recognize him from those sketches?"

"It's one of my hopes," Da Silva said. "Why? Do you have a better idea?"

"No," Wilson admitted. "But I think we—or rather,

you—ought to cover more angles than that. I still think it would be worthwhile putting some men on that Maloca de Tijuca. He used to hang around there quite a bit, and at least it's a smaller area than the whole city of Rio. What harm would it do?"

"No harm at all," Da Silva agreed equably. "In fact, it's a great suggestion. Now all we need is a suggestion as to where we—or rather, I—would get the men to do it. We're more than a little strapped as it is."

"Well, then," Wilson said slowly, "would you mind if I sat around that bar tonight myself? After all, this motorcade you're so worried about takes place tomorrow. . . ."

"The bar," Da Silva asked idly, "or the rooms behind the bar?"

"The bar," Wilson said firmly.

Da Silva studied his friend's face quizzically for several moments and then sighed. "Would it make a lot of difference if I told you I did mind?"

Wilson grinned. "Well, no. . . ."

"Then why ask?" Da Silva suddenly smiled, a rather curious smile, oddly contemplative. His fingers tented, tapping against each other. "As a matter of fact, knowing you, you might just be lucky."

"Lucky? You mean, and run into him?"

"Possibly," Da Silva said. His eyes were steady on Wilson's face. "On the other hand you might be even luckier and not run into him. This man is a killer. I'm sure he's here for an important killing. But I'm equally sure he wouldn't mind tossing in a free one, if the free one happened to be a nosy police officer."

"Worry not," Wilson said, and grinned. "I'll be circumspection itself. Well, take care of the store; I've got to be going. I want to get home and change into my bar clothes."

He opened the door and winked at the seated man. "And don't ruin your eyes with all those reports."

Da Silva grinned back at him. "I won't. And don't ruin your eyes staring at those girls. Or drinking that cheap *pinga*."

The door closed behind Wilson. The smile was wiped instantly from Da Silva's swarthy face. He listened to the receding footsteps until they had disappeared, and then dragged his telephone closer, dialing an internal number. The phone at the other end was lifted instantly.

"Lieutenant Perreira here."

"Perreira? Da Silva. Senhor Wilson just left my office. He'll be coming down in the elevator any moment. I want a man on him—a damned good man. And I want reports as often as possible. I'll either be here or I'll leave word where I can be reached."

Lieutenant Perreira was puzzled. "Senhor Wilson? Of the American Embassy? Your friend? I thought—"

"Don't waste time!" Da Silva said savagely, and slammed the receiver down. He stared at the telephone a few moments in deep thought, organizing his ideas, putting his plans into proper perspective, and then reached for the stack of small photographs once again. The picture of a man's back, a man leaning against the rail, which had caught his attention on his first run-through, was extracted from the pile. He studied it with narrowed eyes a moment, and then reached into his drawer and withdrew the anonymous letter from Salvador de Bahia. It was clipped to the laboratory report he remembered as being quite detailed as to paper source, type of ink, and all the other useless details which had helped him not a bit. He folded the letter and the report, tucked the photograph in among them, and slid the lot into an envelope. This accomplished, he reached for the telephone once again, clicking the button for the central police department operator.

"Hello? This is Captain Da Silva. I want to put through a priority call to Captain Echavarria of the Montevideo police. Instantly! I'll hold on."

His thick fingers drummed impatiently on the desk as he waited; he closed his eyes, resting them, reviewing in his mind the many possibilities, both of error and of success. There were a series of clicks and weird whistles, interspersed at times with various languages, all spoken in that nasal tone which forever identifies the long-distance operators of this world. At long last the interlopers died away; Captain Echavarria came on the line. Da Silva's eyes opened with a visible effort.

"Hello? Hello?"

"Echavarria? Ché, this is Zé Da Silva from Rio—"

"Zé! How goes it?"

"Not good," Da Silva said honestly. "I think we've got trouble here, but there's something you can do to help."

"Anything!" Da Silva could see in his mind's eye his heavyset friend in Montevideo waving one hand enthusiastically as he spoke. "Anything! You know that!"

"Thanks." Da Silva bent over the telephone, speaking quickly. "Here's the story: I'm having an envelope flown down to you. It should be there within two or three hours at the latest. It has a picture in it, and also a letter —hand-written. As well as a laboratory report on the letter, for whatever good it is. This is what I want you to do. . . ."

He spoke for several more minutes. At the other end of the line, Captain Echavarria nodded at regular intervals, one thick hand scribbling down his instructions on a pad.

"I understand. Of course, if the ship has sailed . . ."

"If it sailed, it's in the River Plate on its way to Buenos Aires, or possibly there already. And you'll have to be there anyway. And soon. Because I need the answers by tomorrow morning."

Echavarria stared at the telephone. "By tomorrow morning?"

"That's right," Da Silva said grimly. "And very early tomorrow morning."

Echavarria sighed. "We'll do our best."

"I know you will, and that's good enough for me. Well, I'll hang up and let you get to it."

"And you'll hear from me early tomorrow morning, one way or the other."

"Right. And thanks again, Ché."

"Anytime, Zé. *Ciao.*"

Da Silva placed the telephone back in its cradle and reached out, pressing the button on his desk. Ruy appeared almost at once. Da Silva handed him the envelope. "Ruy. This goes to Captain Echavarria at central police in Montevideo. He must have it within two hours. You will arrange a plane and take it personally. If there is any question about getting the police plane, you will telephone me from Galeão. Is that clear?"

"Right, Captain."

Ruy took the envelope and disappeared. Da Silva smiled at the closed door with genuine affection: one of the best things about the organization he had built up was that they never questioned his instructions. His smile faded; of course, they didn't always carry them out, either. But he knew Ruy would, or would advise him.

He put the thought of Ruy and his errand out of his mind and reached for the telephone once again. This call was going to be the most important of all, and the one which had to be handled just right. It would also be the hardest call of all to get results from. He took a deep breath and dialed the Hotel Gloria; the operator answered at the hotel and then quite routinely connected him to the desired extension. It was obvious from her bored tone that big names no longer served to excite her.

A weary voice answered the extension, speaking in Spanish. *"Alô?"*

Da Silva leaned forward, speaking slowly and clearly. "Hello. I should like to speak personally with Señor Juan Dorcas."

"De parte de quien?"

"I am Captain Da Silva, of the Brazilian police."

There was a slight hesitation. "I'm sorry, Captain, but Señor Dorcas has only just arrived, and is resting. He has left word that he wishes to speak with no one." The speaker made no attempt to sound even faintly sorry.

"And I am equally sorry, señor," Da Silva said with exaggerated politeness, "but I'm afraid the matter is imperative. I'm afraid I must insist on speaking with Señor Dorcas."

The voice at the other end remained suave. "And I am more than equally sorry, señor, but I'm afraid that if you wish to insist, the proper manner is to do it through the Argentinian Embassy." The telephone was firmly disconnected.

Da Silva stared at the instrument in his hand a moment and then hung up. He came to his feet and reached for his jacket, his jaw hardening. It appeared that Señor Juan Dorcas' staff did not understand what Captain Da Silva meant by the word "insist," and this was one time when Da Silva had no intention of being misunderstood. He started for the door and then returned, picking up the telephone for the last time.

"Operator? This is Captain Da Silva. I'm leaving my office. I'll be at the Hotel Gloria until you hear from me again. Yes. In the suite of Señor Juan Dorcas, of Argentina. . . ."

Six

FOR NACIO MADEIRA MENDES, the week that had passed since his return to his beloved Brazil had seemed endless. While he had long since developed the patience necessary for one in his selected profession, he had never developed any patience beyond this. To Nacio, waiting could be tolerated only when it served a purpose, and he was far from convinced that in this case it did. And each day that passed made him more certain that the entire complicated scheme was unnecessary, and that his victim—whoever he might be—would have long since been dispatched had he been left to his own methods.

His daytime hours had been spent in complete boredom, for while he disagreed with his instructions, he still had no intention of jeopardizing his fee by going contrary to them. In addition, it would not have surprised him a bit if Sebastian had put a tail on him to make sure his instructions were carried on during the day. At night, of course, he was under the cold and sterile inspection of Sebastian's girl. As a result life was monotonous. The Zoo, which he visited several times, certainly had no denizen more restless than he, nor one who paced the edges of his cage with more growing frustration.

Nor had the hours spent at the Serrador done anything to ease the situation. While Nacio was by nature a man who could control his emotions, including passion, where it served his purpose, the fact was that he had been without a woman for a long time, and living and sleeping in the same room with Iracema did nothing to help. However, any ideas he might occasionally have had regarding the girl had instantly been scotched by Iracema herself; and although she left a flimsy nightgown on a bathroom hook to be discovered by the room-maid in the morning, she actually slept in a severe pair of slacks and a full blouse, topped off by a long and sexless robe that, together with the uncompromising and slightly superior look in her dark eyes, successfully defied violation.

Many times in those days—and even more in the long and increasingly sleepless nights—Nacio had considered disregarding his instructions to the extent of visiting his old hangout at the Maloca de Tijuca on the beach. He had spent many happy hours there in better times, and for the first time was beginning to appreciate just how happy they had been. Certainly a drink there could do no harm; nor, he was sure, could any of the girls in the rooms back of the bar present any great threat, since they changed frequently, and it was doubtful if any of the old ones would still be around to remember him. Still, it would be a chance, and therefore each time the thought came to him, he thrust it away. Time for these things when the fee was earned and paid. Still, it was a shame. . . .

On the Monday night before the day of the fateful motorcade, Nacio slumped in a soft chair before the television set attempting to concentrate on an old movie that had little to recommend it when it had first been produced by Vitagraph, and had not been improved by its more recent translation into Portuguese. It was no use; he bent over and twiddled with the knob, and was rewarded in quick succession by a woman either explaining or apologizing for a recipe, a busty and brave singer whose élan did not slacken as technicians dragged cables between her and the camera, and a man who kept searching confusedly through a stack of papers before him for the latest news.

It was too much! He leaned down and switched the set off, coming to his feet to prowl the room impatiently. Thank God tomorrow would see an end to this nonsense! His steel-rimmed glasses were on the dresser, as were the uncomfortable cheek-pads; he continually wore his mustache and gloves, and now he scratched at the heavy brush, irritated as always by the itching of the gum arabic, and even more irritated by the difficulty of doing a proper scratching job while wearing surgical gloves.

He glanced at his watch. Where on earth was Iracema? She was usually here long before this; as a matter of fact he normally found her in the room when he returned from having his evening meal. Could anything have happened to her? And, as a result, to the scheme? Which would have made his week of sacrifice a mockery? He shook his head violently, putting the thought aside. If anything were to have happened to the plan, it would have happened before this; nor would he still be free and undisturbed. No; the plan was safe. By now their routine was well-established and accepted at the hotel; on the few times they entered together the room clerk handed them their key automatically, and the elevator operators carried them to their floor without a second glance. Or at least a second glance at him; occasionally their second glances at Iracema had resulted in passing the proper floor.

There was a faint tap at the door, followed in a few seconds by the sound of a key in the lock. He hurriedly slipped his glasses into place and swung about to face the door, his gloved hands jamming themselves into the pockets of his dressing gown. Iracema pushed the door wide, smiling at him brightly, but he knew the smile was really for the benefit of the small bellboy who followed her into the room worshipfully, his arms loaded with gaily wrapped packages all bearing the mark of Mesbla's, the leading department store in the city. The boy placed his load on the bed, accepted his tip and a grateful smile from the girl with a blush that clearly demonstrated which he considered the more valuable, and closed the door softly behind him. Nacio took off his glasses and glared at the girl, his irritation compounded by the fact that her smile had disappeared the moment the door had closed.

"Well?" His voice was harsh. "Where have you been? Out shopping? Is that all you have to do? You were supposed—"

Her abruptly raised hand cut off his complaint. She walked over, swaying, bent and switched on the television set. When the volume had risen enough to form a proper cover for any conversation, she straightened up coolly and looked at him.

"Yes?"

Nacio bit back the anger that automatically rose at the snub. He forced himself to speak calmly. "You were supposed to bring the rifle here tonight."

She tilted her head toward the bed, her eyes mocking. "The gun is in those packages." The sarcasm that tinged her voice brought a slow flush to his sallow face. "I couldn't very well march through the hotel lobby with a rifle on my shoulder."

He disregarded her sarcasm, moving toward the packages. Her voice stopped him.

"And don't unwrap them now. Everything's there; they'll keep until tomorrow. Put them away in the dresser drawer."

"I'll do what I——"

He might just as well have kept silent. Her voice went on, curtly, as it always seemed to be when she spoke to him. "And I'm going to bed. I'm tired."

Nacio clamped his jaws on the angry words that rose in his throat. It was a good thing the affair would be over and done with tomorrow; another day or another night with this—this—iceberg, and he would not want to be responsible for the results. He would either throttle her, or rape her! Or both! Good God, what an impossible woman!

She walked to her suitcase, her full hips swaying as usual, unlocked it and brought out her slacks and robe. Her eyes came up to study him evenly; she might have been looking at a piece of furniture. "And don't play the television too loudly. I want to sleep."

"Wait." The word seemed to come from Nacio's lips without volition. He took a deep breath. "Why do you talk to me the way you do? And look at me the way you do? As if I were some—some animal or something? You're in this business as much as I am!" The anger that had been building in him for days threatened to come to the surface. "Who are you to act so much better than me? Or to act as if Sebastian is so much better than me?"

The expression on her face did not change at all. "Sebastian and you? There is no comparison." She leaned back against the dresser, the robe folded over her arm, pressed against her bosom. "Sebastian is a man. . . ."

"A man?" Nacio stared at her. "Sebastian? Sebastian is a coward, a big, fat, good-looking coward. Who makes a living getting commissions for killing people, and then doesn't have the nerve to do the jobs himself. You call this a man?"

"Yes." Iracema looked at him evenly. "I know he's a coward. That's what makes him a man." For the first time something approximating pity touched her eyes. "You wouldn't understand that."

"I wouldn't."

"You see," she went on slowly, "Sebastian needs me; he can't face problems alone."

Nacio grinned. "For the problems Sebastian faces, he needs me a lot more."

She shook her head slowly. "No. I knew you couldn't understand. And there's more. Sebastian took me from the rooms back of the Maloca de Tijuca over two years ago. He's been good to me. I've been happy with him—"

"The Maloca!" The grin that had crossed the sallow face widened, tinged with evil, and also tinged a bit with anger. "And you sleep in that outfit, and alone?"

Iracema straightened up abruptly, her face hardening. It was evident she was sorry she had ever engaged in the conversation. "That's right. And that's the way it will always be." She disappeared into the bathroom, locking the door firmly behind her.

Nacio stared at the closed panel; the sound of a shower being turned on came to him. A girl from the Maloca de Tijuca and he had slept alone for the past week! The sound of the shower increased; in his mind's eye he could see her stepping out of her clothing, reaching up to push the shower curtain back, and then standing under the streaming water. It was the same picture that had formed in his mind for the past six nights, and it had been bad enough before he had known of her past. Now it was worse.

The sound of the shower stopped. Now she would be stepping out of the tub, her trim body glistening with tiny droplets of water, her hands stretching for a towel to stroke those lush curves, to rub here, to pat there . . . And then she would take a powder puff . . . There was a low growl in his throat at the thought. So great was his concentration on the vision in his mind that the sharp rap on the outer door of the room completely escaped his attention.

The knock on the door was repeated; louder and more insistent this time. He came out of his salacious dream, shaking his head vaguely to clear it, staring at the panel. Someone at the door? But who? He frowned; it was probably only the bellboy, inventing some idiotic excuse to see the lady of the room again. But still . . . He walked over and placed his head next to the panel.

"Who's there?"

"Open up!"

No bellboy ever spoke in those tones, not to guests! His eyes narrowed instantly, swinging about the room as if seeking some means of escape; his hand reached automatically to the spot beneath his belt where a revolver would have been under standard conditions. The rap was repeated impatiently. He willed himself to calmness, thinking furiously.

"One moment . . ."

The steel-rimmed glasses were snatched from the dresser top and thrust into place; there was no time for the cheek-pads, which were swept into his pocket. He reached for the door and then realized he still had his gloves on. With a muttered curse he dragged them off and jammed them into his pocket on top of the cheek-pads.

He'd have to worry about fingerprints some other time. He took a deep breath and opened the door.

Two men stood in the opening confronting him, both bulky and with the unmistakable appearance of plain-clothes police. Nacio had seen them often enough in the past to recognize the type instantly. For an instant panic almost gripped him, but then he realized that had he been recognized they would not be standing there; they would be grappling with him. The thought eased his tension a bit, but he remained wary with the experience of years. The eyes of the larger of the two men studied him almost curiously, and then dropped to refer to a sheet of paper in his hand. He looked up again.

"Dr. Carabello?"

"Yes?" He tried to make his voice normal, noncommittal, but despite himself it came out harsh, suspicious. "What is it?"

The man in front shouldered his way into the room. He held out a billfold opened to display an identification card, and then flipped it shut before Nacio could even study it, and thrust it into a hip pocket. "Sergeant Ramos. Police. Do you mind if we look around?"

Nacio's jaw tightened. "Look around? For what?"

The detective stared at him with suddenly narrowing eyes; the reaction of this particular hotel guest was certainly different from the others he had checked that evening. He motioned abruptly to his partner, who came farther into the room, taking up a position that effectively blocked the doorway. Nacio realized his previous tone had been a mistake; he changed it, attempting to merely sound aggrieved. "What's this all about?"

"It started out as just routine." The black expressionless eyes were studying him evenly, but the hunched shoulders and the readiness of the large hands indicated suspicion. "I don't know where it will end." Ramos turned away, moving over to stand beside the bed, staring down at the packages there. "We'll want to see what's in those, and check out the rest of your things as well."

Nacio's body tensed. Damn that idiot Sebastian and his refusal to allow him a revolver! And damn his own stupidity in wasting time talking to the girl when he should have been assembling the rifle! At least with a weapon there might have been a chance to shoot his way to safety, instead of being trapped! Sergeant Ramos continued to contemplate the sallow face before him with hard suspicion.

"And, of course, we'll want to see your *carteira de identidade*."

There was the loud rasp of a bolt being slid back, and the bathroom door opened. All three men swung around at the sound. In the opening Iracema stood, her eyes squeezed shut, her fingers rubbing them. "Darling, I've gotten some soap in my eyes. Could you——?"

The light behind her outlined her lush figure through the sheer nightgown; the deep slash at the neckline made no attempt to contain her full breasts. Nacio's eyes widened.

"Darling——?" Iracema opened one eye to squint at him and then for the first time seemed to notice the two strangers in the room. With a feminine squeal she attempted to cover her charms as best she could, and then retreated in confusion, closing the bathroom door sharply behind her. Nacio turned, dazed, to find the two men grinning at him in a knowing manner. The larger of the two backed to the doorway, drawing his partner with him.

"I'm very sorry, *Doutor*. I hope you'll forgive us. I don't believe it will be necessary to take up any more of your time. Or that of your—ah—your senhora." The other winked at him almost envyingly, and pulled the door closed behind them. Nacio dropped on the bed closest to him and rubbed his hand almost wearily over his face.

This time when the bathroom door opened, Iracema appeared in her usual nightgarb, covered as usual by the long robe. She walked to her bed and turned down the thin top cover, lay down, and drew it to her chin. When she spoke one might have thought there had been no incident with two detectives a few moments before. Her tone also closed the door on any further personal confidences.

"You can turn off the main light; the lamp is sufficient for the television. And keep the volume down. I'm tired and I want to get some sleep." She looked up at him a moment calculatingly. "And you'd better get some sleep, too. We both have a busy day tomorrow, and it has to go right." She rolled over and closed her eyes.

Nacio stared down at her. Sleep! After the narrow escape they had just had, not to mention the memory of that lovely vision standing in the bathroom doorway, made even more enticing for not having been completely nude? Sleep! The woman wasn't human! His jaw tightened. Well, he was! He reached out, twitching the thin cover from the girl, reaching for the neck of the blouse beneath the robe. Iracema rolled over instantly, facing him; her eyes were icy. In her hand was a long needle that had been concealed at her side.

There was a moment's silence. Then Nacio growled low in his throat and turned blindly toward the door. His hand was on the knob when Iracema spoke.

"Where are you going?"

He looked back at her a moment without answering, opened the door, and closed it softly behind him. . . .

From the bumpy sand road that led from the Gavea bridge along the deserted beach to terminate in the Maloca de Tijuca, the dim but gaily colored lanterns that gave the wide palm-studded grove an air of festivity, illuminated the huge three-sided compound of the *maloca* which was augmented by the soft, pulse-catching rhythm of a current carnival favorite coming from the largest of the thatched huts. Wilson, swinging his car through the wide vine-covered gates of the compound, felt amazed as always when he found himself in similar places that the outskirts of Rio de Janeiro offer. Here there was a feeling of being deep in the interior, far from any vestige of civilization, and yet just across the curved beach that formed the fourth side of the compound the lights of Copacabana beach twinkled in the distance, in competition to the eerie reflections of moonbeams dusting the tips of the low rippling waves that ran up to wash one edge of the clearing.

A lovely place, Wilson thought sincerely, and swung his ancient car around in the almost-empty parking lot to allow it to point outward and in the direction of the gate, should the necessity arise for a rapid departure. Not the most moral place in the world, the Maloca de Tijuca, he admitted to himself, but certainly one of the loveliest of the immoral places. Which may or may not explain its popularity among so many of the married men in this town, he added to himself with an inner smile. They may all be aesthetes, searching for beauty, he thought; and in a place like this, if you don't find it in one place, you may in another.

He switched off the ignition, descended, and was about

to lock the car when he thought better of it. Rather—and against all the tendencies so firmly ingrained in a Rio inhabitant—he even reached back and reinserted his key in the ignition slot. This action may, he conceded to himself, possibly cost me an automobile; on the other hand it might just save my life. Which, he added to himself with a smile, was a toss-up in values here in Brazil. He closed the door and walked lightheartedly toward the muted music coming from the largest of the thatched huts.

On the dim road just outside of the Maloca, Detective First Grade Pedro Armando Freire slowed down, nodded in satisfaction, and then continued to drive a few hundred yards farther along. The bumpy road ended in a rough circle; he swung about it so that his car was aimed once again in the direction of the city, eased the vehicle off the road into the blacker shadows beneath a thick stand of palm, and turned off the ignition.

Detective Freire found it difficult to understand why anyone would want to trail a man to a place like the Maloca, since his purpose in coming here could only be one, but on the other hand he had to admit that it was an easy assignment. The best thing, of course, was that a person could only leave on the one bumpy road, coming through the gate he could see so clearly, which made trailing him a cinch. And, too, the music coming faintly from the compound was pleasant, and the breeze from the nearby ocean refreshing after the heat of the day.

He leaned back comfortably, prepared to enjoy his wait, and then leaned forward again, frowning. There was the sound of someone scuffling through the sand, coming across the dunes that separated the beach from the main highway. His frown deepened; anyone who came to the Maloca always came by car. He began to sit straighter and then leaned back again, chiding himself. The help, of course, would not be blessed with cars; they would naturally come to work by omnibus and cross the dunes from the main road as the shortest way to work. His theory was substantiated a moment later, for the shadowy figure that slipped across the road made no attempt to use the main gate but walked silently along the compound wall to disappear down the far side in the direction of the beach. Detective Freire knew there was a small doorway there for the use of employees, and he relaxed again, pleased both with his proper deduction and with its rapid confirmation. His fingers tapped out the quick rhythm of the music on the steering wheel as he waited patiently for his quarry to reappear.

His quarry, in the meantime, had entered the larger of the group of thatched huts. He was not surprised to find but one couple dancing in the dim room; the parking lot had suggested to him that the place would not be crowded. He seated himself at a table as far as possible from the large, exotic jukebox and waited for the bartender to note his presence, watching in the meanwhile the easy rhythm of the closely pressed couple. Their smooth execution of the dance evinced from him admiration, as well as a touch of envy. Wilson had been in the country many years and had mastered most of its mysteries, but the effortless ease with which a Brazilian danced the samba continued to evade him. There was a diffident cough at his elbow and he looked up to find the bartender waiting patiently at his side. Wilson smiled genially at the white-jacketed man.

"Dull tonight, eh?"

The bartender nodded, bending over to wipe the already spotless table. "Every Monday. I don't know why they stay open on Mondays. . . ." There was a touch of bitterness in his voice. He seemed to be saying that he did, indeed, know why they stayed open on Mondays; it was a vicious move on the part of a heartless management designed to see to it that he had only one day a week off, rather than two. He straightened up, dismissing his ill-fortune. "The senhor is expecting someone?"

"No," Wilson said. "I'm alone."

The bartender sighed. "The kitchen is closed."

"I didn't come for dinner," Wilson said.

The bartender nodded, the usual formalities completed. "And what kind of girl does the senhor prefer?"

Wilson smiled at him. "Nor, tonight, did I come for a girl. What I would really like is a drink. An imported cognac. Preferably Maciera Five-Star, if you have it."

The bartender stared at him intently for a moment, and then shrugged. There were, of course, mentally twisted people who got their kicks out of just visiting a place like this, although this one certainly didn't look like one of those. It just went to prove that you never could tell. "Maciera Five-Star? I'll see. If I don't have any here, there may be some at the other bar, in the back."

"Thank you," Wilson said, and leaned back.

The bartender returned to his province, verified his stocks and discovered, as he had suspected, that Maciera Five-Star was not among them. He automatically checked the room before leaving; the couple glued together near the jukebox did not look as if they would require his services for awhile, if ever. He wiped his hands on his apron and pushed through the door that led to the deserted kitchen and thence to a second bar that was called upon on such busy nights as Fridays and Saturdays. He opened the door to the dimly lit room and then stopped, glaring. Some intruder was in the process of removing a bottle from one of the shelves.

"Hey, you! You're not supposed to be in here!" He modified his tone a bit as the man turned. The owners were particular about how one addressed a guest, even a guest who was out of line. And this man was dressed as a guest might be dressed, and not as a sneak-thief. "I'm sorry, sir. This bar is closed. If you want service . . ."

His visitor frowned at him a moment. He was a medium-sized man with a heavy mustache, who was wearing steel-rimmed glasses. One hand came up to remove the glasses while two fingers of the other masked the mustache for a moment. The bartender's eyes widened incredulously; he gasped.

"Nacio! What on earth—!"

Nacio glared at him. "Louder!" he growled savagely. "I wouldn't want anyone out there not to hear you!"

The bartender dutifully lowered his voice. "I'm sorry, it was the shock. . . . What on earth are you doing here in Rio? I thought—I mean, I heard you were in Portugal."

"I am," Nacio said. He turned and brought the bottle closer, reached for a glass and poured himself a drink.

"And how did you get here? I didn't hear you drive in."

"A fairy godmother brought me." Nacio drank and then gestured with his head. "From the highway. By bus." The taste of the liquor was pleasant to him; the rich warmth of his choice spread through his body almost at once. How stupid of Sebastian to ban a drink! Which reminded him— He set down his glass and looked at the other calculatingly.

"I need a gun."

"A gun?" The bartender wiped his hands against his apron; they had begun to sweat. "Look, Nacio, I don't want any trouble. And besides, I don't have—"

"You have a revolver under the bar out there," Nacio said coldly. "You always had one there, and I'm sure you still have. And if you don't want any trouble, don't argue.

Go in there and get it for me." He smiled faintly. "Don't worry; I'll see that your boss gets paid for it."

"But I keep that gun just in case—"

"Consider this 'in case'!" Nacio's voice was beginning to tinge with anger. He poured himself another drink, threw it down his throat, and jerked his head in the general direction of the wall. "Who's out there?"

The bartender shrugged helplessly. "Just one couple, dancing—one of the girls and a fellow comes in here to see her regularly. And a single, some oddball. You know how dead it is here on a Monday."

"An oddball?" Nacio's eyes narrowed; he set his empty glass down on the bar slowly. "What do you mean?"

"Just what I said. A character. He's alone, doesn't expect anyone, doesn't want a girl . . ." He suddenly remembered what had brought him here. "He wants Maciera Five-Star. Ah, here it is!"

Nacio's hand clamped on his arm. "What does he look like?"

"How do I know what he looks like? Go into the kitchen—"

But Nacio had already dropped his arm and had slipped through the door to the kitchen. He slid back the door of the service hatchway the merest fraction and peered through it. Wilson, facing him across the room, was given a minute inspection. Nacio frowned and reached for the bartender's arm once again as that one came through, bearing a bottle in one hand.

"How long has he been here?" It was a taut whisper.

"Ten minutes. Maybe five."

"I see." Nacio stood thinking a moment, and then made up his mind. "You go out there and give him his drink. And then bring me back the gun. And after that—"

"Yes?"

"After that you manage to go outside and find out what he's driving."

"But why?" The bartender was almost wailing. Three years this Nacio had been out of Rio, and now he had to come back on his shift! Why couldn't he have returned when one of the other bartenders was on duty? "Look, Nacio, I don't want any trouble."

Nacio's jaw tightened; his eyes glinted dangerously. "Then you'll do what you're told!" He pushed the other man brusquely. "Now, get going!"

Through the thin slit in the hatchway opening he watched the bartender pause at the bar, pour a drink shakily, and carry it over to Wilson's table. He came back, wiping his hands furiously, and with an exaggerated air of innocence picked the revolver from beneath the bar and hid it under his apron. Nacio, watching him, seethed inwardly. Had anyone been paying attention, the idiot would certainly have been discovered! He waited until the bartender had come back through the kitchen door and then jerked the revolver from the reluctant hand that held it timidly forward. He checked it and stuffed it beneath his belt, and then buttoned his jacket tightly over the slight bulge. He jerked his head.

"Now I want to know what he's driving."

"But—"

"And don't argue!"

The bartender shook his head in resignation, and slowly went back to the bar. He glanced about and then walked to the open doorway leading to the patio, attempting to appear casual; one cavernous yawn and he stepped out into the warm darkness. Through the slit in the hatchway window Nacio's eyes flickered over the dancing couple and then returned to study the man sipping cognac at the other table.

Nacio frowned. A man alone in a place like this, who neither brought his own bed-partner nor requested one from the management—that in itself was quite unusual. And a man who managed to arrive so conveniently just a few moments before he himself did. His eyes ran over the relaxed figure. Certainly innocuous enough to outward appearance, and looking almost too harmless, and yet there was something about the man that led Nacio to believe he was actually neither. He nodded his head in growing conviction; this was exactly the type a *miserável* like Sebastian would use to follow and check up on him. The heavyset *filho de mãe* would have enough brains to pick someone he assumed Nacio would never suspect. Iracema had undoubtedly notified Sebastian the moment he had left the hotel room, and where was the first place someone would be sent to find him? The Maloca, of course!

Except for one little thing, Nacio thought, a cruel smile creasing his thin lips: they are still only looking for me. They haven't found me yet!

The bartender wandered in from the compound as vaguely as he had wandered out, and managed to reach the kitchen without actually breaking into a sprint. Nacio cast his eyes toward the ceiling imploringly, and then returned them to the white face before him.

"Well?"

The bartender took a deep breath. "He's driving a Chevrolet, only five or six years old. Practically new. It's turned around so it points at the gate. And it isn't locked." His voice betrayed his shock; he didn't know what Nacio was so upset about, but he had to admit that this leaving a car unlocked in Rio de Janeiro was certainly a most suspicious circumstance. Especially one that was practically new. He looked at Nacio a bit slyly and then delivered his *pièce de résistance*. "And he's left his keys in the ignition!"

Nacio nodded; he was not surprised. It was the only explanation that covered all the facts. Well! So Sebastian wanted to play games, did he? He smiled faintly, leaning forward.

"Now, look—this man will be wanting another drink soon. He's planning on waiting here as long as he has to. So when he orders, you will serve him his Maciera. But in it you will put a knockout drop."

The bartender opened his mouth to deny that a respectable establishment like the Maloca de Tijuca had such potions, and then closed it. Some other time and to some other person, but not to Nacio Mendes! He cleared his throat nervously. "And then you will steal his car?"

"Then," Nacio said quietly, "I shall not steal his car. Then I shall leave you alone. Without even visiting your little playmates in the back." His unhappiness at this turn of events was evident in his voice.

"But what will I do with him? He'll fall on the floor! I can't . . ."

Nacio thought quickly. "You will tuck him into his own car; you said it was unlocked. And then?" He shrugged humorously. "Forget about him. You close up at four. Go home and let the man who opens up in the morning worry about him."

"But—"

The light humor that had appeared on Nacio's face disappeared as quickly as it had come. "I said . . ." He paused, listening, and then glanced through the slit in the hatchway. Wilson was tapping in a polite manner on the table with the edge of his glass. Nacio turned back. "He wants another drink. You know what to do."

He pushed the unhappy bartender toward the door, and then watched through his peephole. When the drink was finally delivered to Wilson's table, it was done with far less nervousness than Nacio had feared, but then he remembered that the serving of knockout drops was not a rare occurrence at the Maloca. Quite often it was the only means of maintaining the peace and quiet so necessary to a respectable establishment of its kind, and the bartenders had all learned long since the most efficient manner of serving them.

Nacio watched with satisfaction as the drink slowly began to take effect. The sudden startled yawn, the rubbing of the eyes, the rather shocked blinking in a concentrated effort to focus—all spoke well for the effectiveness of the potion. He grinned down at the bartender, who had returned to his side.

"And one last thing—a note I want you to put in his pocket."

He dug a pencil from an inner pocket of his jacket and looked about the kitchen for paper. An order pad lying on the serving pantry served; he tore a sheet loose, turned it over, and carefully printed a few words on the reverse side. He reread them with a grin, folded the slip and handed it to the white-jacketed man at his side. "You'll tuck this in his pocket when he passes out. And make sure it doesn't fall out when you put him in his car."

The bartender stared at him reproachfully, as having interjected an unnecessary problem into his otherwise normal Monday chores. "I can't handle him alone. Not into his car."

Nacio's grin was wiped away instantly. "I said—"

"But I can't!" The stubbornness of the bartender's tone indicated that he had gone as far as he was going, and that no threats could increase his strength. Nacio studied him with narrowed eyes and then gave in, albeit far from graciously.

"All right, then! I'll help you with him. You get him to

the doorway and I'll meet you there, outside." He glanced through the peephole once again. "And you'd better get out there before our friend really *does* fall on the floor."

In his car in the black shadows of the palm grove, Detective Freire was beginning to get restless. He took a deep drag on the cigarette cupped in his hand and brought the glowing ash next to the dial of his wristwatch. A sigh escaped him. He hoped the American he was trailing was not one to spend the entire night at his pleasures. Not only was there no telephone available in the vicinity from which to call in his reports, but there was also no place around where he could get a *cafezinho*. He glanced about. There could be no harm in stretching his legs; he could always hear a car start from within the compound in plenty of time to get back behind his steering wheel.

He opened the car door, swung himself to the sandy road, and softly closed the door behind him. A beautiful night, he thought to himself, and walked quietly toward the entrance to the Maloca compound. From the shadows beside the gate he would be able to see the exotically colored lanterns and hear the music more clearly; in addition there was also the chance he might catch a glimpse of his quarry, and from that glimpse possibly even manage some conclusion as to his intentions for the rest of the evening.

He came to the entrance, glanced ahead a moment along the deserted road leading to the city, and then peered into the compound. For a moment he stared, frowning, puzzled, before he realized he was actually seeing two men helping—or rather, dragging—a third toward a car parked at an angle along one wall. His eyes studied the scene suspiciously, swung to the car in question, and then narrowed instantly and dangerously. The man being pulled senselessly between the other two was his quarry! His hand dove for his revolver, bringing it out; he stepped out into the clearing, advancing cautiously toward the trio grouped near the car door.

"You men!"

Nacio swung his head about, startled; the bartender gasped and released his hold on Wilson, who slid unconscious to the ground, his head resting against one tire. Detective Freire came closer, slowly gesturing with his gun.

"Step back. Farther. Against the car. Now turn around and lean on the fender."

The bartender was making hysterical little sounds deep in his throat; he swung about hastily and bent over the worn metal, cursing the day he had ever met Nacio Mendes. Nacio continued to stand there, looking at the detective apologetically.

"I don't know who you are, sir, or what business you have interfering, but you don't understand. This man . . ."

Freire raised his gun slightly. "This is police business. And we'll talk about it when you've turned around. Move!"

A flame of pure fury swept Nacio, though no sign of it showed on his tense, pale face. So Sebastian had not only been stupid enough to put a watchdog on him, but a watchdog the police were following! A watchdog that brought the police to him! The utter, vicious, miserable fool! He forced himself to calmness, to even hazard a deprecating smile.

"You still don't understand, officer. This man took sick—"

Freire shook his head in impatience and moved forward, jamming his gun into Nacio's stomach. It was a mistake, and one which would have been a great disappoint-

ment to his instructor at the Police Academy. A sudden
twist and Freire found his gun arm locked, the weapon
pointing uselessly behind his opponent, and the sharp
pungent breath of Nacio in his face. A second later he felt
the painful pressure of a second revolver pushing against
his own stomach. The voice from the face inches from his
own was icy and flat.

"Drop your gun!"

Freire's fingers loosened his weapon; it fell without a
sound to the ground. Nacio stepped back quickly, his own
revolver steady, speaking harshly over his shoulder.

"You! Idiot! Stop leaning against the car and get our
watchdog friend into it!" He stared with cruel satisfaction
into the veiled eyes of the detective. "And you. You're going for a walk with me. Along the beach. . . ."

The bartender paused in his task of raising the inert
body of Wilson, raising horrified eyes. "Nacio! No!"

"Shut up!"

There was an unconscious gasp from Detective Freire;
his eyes widened as he stared at the spectacled and mustached face before him. Nacio grinned at him viciously.
"So you recognize me, eh? Don't worry, my friend. It
wouldn't have saved you even if you hadn't. . . ."

Nacio inserted the key in the lock and opened the door
with the maximum of caution, glancing in. Iracema, still
in her robe, was sitting in a chair facing the door; her head
had fallen forward, her steady breathing indicating that
sleep had interrupted her vigil. With a faint grin, Nacio
tiptoed into the room and softly closed the door behind
him; the small lamp the girl had left lit furnished him all
the illumination he needed. He slid the revolver from its
hiding place beneath his belt and placed it inside the top
dresser drawer with care; the faint odor of cordite dis-

appeared as he slid it shut. He silently began to undress.

He lowered himself cautiously onto the bed and slid beneath the thin top cover. Iracema's breathing changed slightly, as if disturbed by some sound or sleeping thought, and then returned to its steady cadence. Nacio grinned at the still figure a moment; his adventure of the evening had acted as a tonic, sharpening his nerves for the task of the following day.

He smiled faintly and closed his eyes. So Sebastian had wanted to play games, eh? Fortunately, at the game of killing, he was the expert, or it might not have turned out so well. The pleasant thought remained with him for the few moments it took him to fall asleep.

Seven

TUESDAY dawned clear and warm; from the window of the eighth-floor room at the Hotel Serrador the view was of unalloyed beauty. The Beira Mar drive and the curving bay framing the mountains in the background both sparkled with the combined efforts of a bountiful nature and an active Rio street-cleaning department. Nacio, standing there in his dressing gown, watched a city truck slowly make its way along the drive, pausing at suitable intervals to place down sections of wooden barricades which scurrying workmen instantly lined up along the curbs. Traffic was apparently being diverted from the drive south of the Hotel Gloria; the route selected for the motorcade lay bare under the growing heat of the bright sun. Nacio smiled grimly, nodding in satisfaction. The arena for his dramatic act was being prepared as well as if he were directing the operation himself.

He turned from the window, returning to the gun he

had just finished assembling, picking it up and caressing it once again. It was, indeed, a beauty. It seemed to him as he slid his hands over the stock almost sensuously, that it was even more lovely than when he had first handled it at Sebastian's house. The balance was perfect; the fine-grained wood had been polished by some previous loving owner until its patina gave the surface the smooth feeling of glass, or of soft skin. He slid the telescopic sight into place and locked it, and then stood well back in the shadows of the room, raising the gun, bringing it to bear on the War Memorial.

The angular modern figures postured in frozen metal before the gaunt tower of the memorial sprang into sudden sharp outline; an overalled workman, sweeping the broad patio in a last-minute bit of housekeeping, seemed to be but inches from his eye. Nacio's gloved fingers touched a knurled knob, bringing the cross-hairs into focus. He lowered the sight slightly, bringing the sight to bear on a tattered breast-pocket of the blue denim coverall, following it evenly as it swayed in unconscious rhythm with the movement of the broom. The gloved finger tightened ever so slightly on the trigger and then relaxed. With a smile he lowered the gun, nodding to himself. With that clarity of light, and with that excellent equipment, he knew there wouldn't be the slightest problem in completing his assignment successfully.

Behind him, Iracema watched his performance through the mirror of the dressing table. Her cheeks were still slightly flushed with anger as she recalled waking with a stiff neck to find the missing Nacio snoring, a beatific smile upon his face. She thrust the thought aside and completed her toilet, dabbing lightly at the corners of her full lips with a bit of tissue. Time enough for explanations when the three of them were all together at

Sebastian's after the event. Her hand paused in the act of discarding the tissue; after the event, what Nacio had done the night before would matter little. They would each take their share and disband, and the tensions of the past week would soon be forgotten in the vast horizons that would open with that much money at their disposal.

She swung about on her stool, studying the man before her. Nacio met her eye squarely, grinning. He was quite aware that she attributed his cheerfulness to a liaison the evening before that had not—unfortunately—occurred; he was also aware that, for some unknown reason, there seemed to be a bit more feeling in her eyes. He was, however, astute enough to suspect it had nothing to do with him as an individual, but only reflected her growing anxiety regarding the job as the moment of accomplishment finally approached.

She looked at him steadily. "How do you feel?"

His grin widened. With the gun in his hands he seemed a different man, more assured, less affected by her presence. "If you mean am I nervous, the answer is no. This isn't my first job, you know."

"I know." Her eyes studied him evenly. "But it's the most important job you've ever done."

He looked at her sardonically. "To the men I've killed, all of my jobs have been of equal importance."

"And to you?"

"To me?" He shrugged. "To me they've been of equal unimportance. To me a job is a job."

"Except that this one pays more money than you ever dreamed of."

"I know. And I'm sure it will also pay you and Sebastian more than you ever dreamed of, as well."

"It will." She came to her feet rather abruptly, as if indicating that that phase of the discussion was ended. Her eyes studied the room carefully. "I'm going now. I've got everything I want in my purse; the rest of my things stay here. You'd better start getting ready yourself."

"I'll be ready."

She opened her mouth to say something and then closed it. She reached for her purse. "I'll call you from the Gloria as soon as the motorcade leaves, to tell you which car he's in, and in which seat. Be sure to keep the telephone free. . . ."

Nacio looked at her with a faint smile. And who's nervous now? He hadn't used the telephone since they had been there, and obviously wouldn't be using it at such a crucial moment. Iracema colored slightly as she read his thought, but chose to disregard it. "And don't forget the television. Any program except—"

"I know. Any program except music." He laid the gun on the bed and straightened up. "You'd better be going."

"Yes." She moved toward the door and then paused. "And the knob; wipe it off on your way out. And be sure to put out the sign for the maid not to disturb you." She hesitated a moment, as if torn by the desire to repeat all of the instructions once again, and then forced herself to refrain. Her eyes came up.

"Good luck." The door closed quickly behind her.

Nacio stared after her with a faint sneer on his lips. Good luck! Somehow it was the wrong thing to say. As a professional assassin he gave small thought to the problems of his victim, but it still struck him as being out of place to wish good luck for a killing. And besides, luck didn't enter into it; it was strictly a matter of skill.

He sighed thoughtfully. Maybe it was just as well that nothing had come of their spending almost a week together in the same room; even with her cooperation it would probably have been like going to bed with a

piranha. In a way he felt sorry for Sebastian; that maternal
feeling of hers would one day swallow him up. Still, that
was Sebastian's problem and not his. His problem was to
do the job properly and get away with a whole skin; wait
until the excitement had died down, and then figure out
how to spend that fabulous fee. Which shouldn't be any
harder than the killing itself, he thought with a grin.
Certainly no harder than the killing the previous evening,
and that had been no problem at all. The one with the
problem would be Sebastian; his share of the fee would
buy him the girl.

With a shake of his head at the thought of the strange
people one was forced to associate with in the course of a
job, he slipped out of his dressing gown and slowly began
to dress.

The crowds were forming two and three deep about the
low wooden barricades; military police in their faded
brown uniforms and their oversized helmets were stationed every twenty or thirty yards along the inside of the
barrier, facing each other at rigid parade rest, their hands
locked behind them, but within easy reach of their hol-
stered guns. From the recessed window above, Nacio
studied the scene, his eyes carefully calculating distances
and potential problems. Between the hotel and the Beira
Mar stretched the Praça Paris, a green band of foliage and
formal gardens; a few trees at the southern end of the
Praça blocked portions of his view of the route, and the
same held true of sections to the north of the War Memorial. But the important part of the route was open; those
vital yards that stretched to the immediate sides of the
stark structure. He clenched and unclenched his fists, relaxing his fingers, staring down thoughtfully. A television
truck passed slowly along the deserted avenue, its camera

weaving from the roof like the antennae of some strange monster searching out prey.

Nacio glanced at his watch. Ten o'clock—Iracema should be calling very soon. His hand patted his jacket pocket; his glasses were in place. His cheek-pads were also in place, a bit uncomfortable, but necessary to save time at the moment of his departure. A glance about the room assured him that all was in order according to the plan; he nodded and wandered to the window, frowning down. The crowds had increased at the barricades, and cars were beginning to pull to the curb of the adjoining drive, prepared to risk the displeasure of the police in order to see the visiting delegates at close hand.

The telephone suddenly rang. Nacio walked to the nightstand, reaching for the instrument. A small electric current touched his nerves, the tingle of anticipation that always prefaced a job; it passed in the same moment and he brought the instrument to his ear, not at all surprised by his own composure.

"Hello? Irace—"

A heavy, deep voice cut in, anxiety apparent in its tone. "Hello? Is this Dr. Carabello?"

The unexpectedness of the voice wiped away Nacio's smugness in an instant; his fingers tightened on the cold plastic. His voice was harsh. "Who's this?" Who on earth could it be? What could have happened to Iracema that another was calling in her place? Any trouble at this late date could spell disaster.

The voice at the other end hurried on, anxious to avoid interruption, to save time. "This is the *portaria* of the hotel. We have a very sick man in the hotel, a guest—on your floor, actually—and we've called an ambulance, but I'm sure the senhor realizes how long they delay, and since the poor man is only a few doors away from your room, we were wondering if you might be so kind—"

"A sick man?" He stared at the telephone, honestly puzzled. A sick man? What on earth did he have to do with sick men? Why come to him with sick men? Especially in this crucial moment when Iracema would be telephoning from the *Gloria*?

"A very sick man, I'm afraid." On this point the deep voice was positive. "And since you happen to be the only doctor registered in the hotel at the moment, we thought . . ." The voice trailed off, its message completed.

Nacio nodded. Of course; he was supposed to be a doctor. An idiot idea in the first place, but too late to do anything about that now. Now the only thing was to get this pest off the telephone, and fast!

"I'm sorry," he said brusquely, still irritated by the unexpected call. "I'm afraid I'm not that kind of a doctor. I'm a—" He paused, thinking rapidly. What kind of a doctor could he be and still safely refuse to treat a sick man? The first thought that came to him was of a veterinarian, but somehow his pride would not allow it. Fortunately a substitute occurred to him before his pause might seem suspicious to the other. "I'm a dentist, senhor."

Disappointment fought with apology in the other's voice. "A dentist? Then I'm very sorry we troubled you, *Doutor*. Unless, of course, you happen to be acquainted with a medical man . . ."

"I'm sorry. I know no one in Rio." Nacio set the telephone firmly in place. And there was even a bit of luck connected with that, he suddenly thought—if the man had been suffering from an infected tooth, I would have been on that blasted phone for another ten minutes trying to get out of it! He started to smile at the thought and then hurriedly picked up the telephone as it rang again.

Iracema's voice came on, low and bitter in its denunciation. "You fool! You . . . you . . . you *irresponsável!* You were told not to use the telephone! I've been calling . . ."

"Save it," Nacio said wearily. "It was the *portaria*. They called me. They thought—"

"Never mind who called who! We've wasted enough time as it is. The motorcade must be halfway there by now." It suddenly occurred to Nacio that her anger was actually motivated by nervousness; that the girl was close to hysterics. Amateurs, he thought with disgust, and paid close attention to her words. "The man you want is sitting in the second car of the *fila*. There's a motorcycle escort first, and then a television camera truck, and then the line of cars. He's in the second one, an open Cadillac, black. He's in the back seat, on the side toward the bay. Do you understand?"

Nacio nodded. "What does he look like?"

"There's no time for descriptions. The second car, back seat, on the side of the bay—the side away from you. Is that clear?"

"The second car in the *fila* after the television truck, a black Cadillac, open; the back seat—"

He was talking to a dial tone. He set the instrument back into its cradle and moved quickly to the window. The procession was plainly in view, slowly approaching the War Memorial from behind the curtain of foliage that screened the southern approaches of the Beira Mar. The wind caught the high wail of the police sirens, carrying it on the breeze in undulating waves to his window. He nodded and dragged one of the large armchairs from its accustomed place before the television set, swinging it beside the bed. The wide back would serve as an excellent steady for his arm when he fired the shot.

He dropped to the bed and reached for the rifle before he suddenly remembered the television. He came to his feet; two steps and he had twisted the small knob. He waited with growing impatience for the set to warm up, his eyes moving between the blank eye of the screen and the open window with its distant view of the approaching motorcade. There was the sudden sound of a pistol shot; despite himself he flinched. The picture tube came alive, accompanied by the sound of thudding fists and the blur of men fighting in a saloon. He nodded in profound satisfaction and adjusted the volume higher; exactly the proper program for the purpose, and a good omen. Which is always a pleasant thing, he thought, and returned to the bed and the rifle.

The armchair served perfectly, as he had checked before; it allowed just the right angle without being uncomfortable. He rested one elbow on it and slowly brought the loaded rifle into position, peering along the foreshortened barrel in the direction of the distant barricades with their crowds of people. They wanted a show, and for those hundreds directly before the Memorial, he would provide them with one they would never forget! The telescopic sight was almost at proper adjustment; the policemen on the escorting motorcycles leaped into the eyepiece, their vehicles appearing to be stunted by the distorted depth of focus, their handlebars weaving awkwardly at the unaccustomed slow pace. Their intent expressions were clearly discernible before the stark framing of the outer cross-hairs.

The motorcycle policeman in the lead suddenly raised a gloved hand commandingly, and in the same motion veered slightly toward the curb; other motorcycles appeared beside him, pulling up, feet braking their slow motion against the pavement. The motorcade had begun to arrive at the War Memorial.

Nacio nuzzled the gun against his cheek, drawing comfort from its smoothness, moving it slowly in a brief arc to encompass the cars behind the escort. The best time, of course, would be as the motorcade paused at the curb, and the delegates prepared to step down to attend the ceremony. As they rose to leave their cars, the man he wanted would make a perfect target.

His eye noted the first car behind the television truck—an eight-passenger Chrysler, dark blue in color, probably rented by the Foreign Office for the occasion from some funeral parlor. The telescopic sight inspected its occupants briefly; a momentary feeling of omnipotence clutched him. Consider this, he said silently to the men in the dark Chrysler: were you the ones I was paid to kill, even now you would be slumping against the side of the car, blind to the startled milling of the crowd, deaf to the confusion. But you are fortunate; the man I want is not in your car. Still, he thought suddenly, every man's head lies in the cross-hairs of some hidden weapon, and none of us avoids the shot forever. . . .

The round circle of his tubular view moved slowly to the second car. It was, indeed, a black Cadillac, and Nacio's lips twisted grimly. Now that the moment was upon him, he seemed in the grip of some cold, inexorable force, directing his movements, controlling even his thoughts. The black cross-hairs crept past the hood of the Cadillac; the driver came into view, one hand shifting the gear lever, the fingers of the other tightening on the wheel as he turned toward the curb. Nacio's fingers tightened slightly on the trigger of the gun as he started to ease the weapon in the direction of the occupants in the rear seat.

The figure on his side of the car was gesticulating, his back hunched; Nacio disregarded him and touched the nob of the sight ever so slightly, shifting the rifle to follow the slow movement of the car. Now was the time! He brought the sight to bear on the right breast pocket of his victim's jacket; his finger tightening steadily on the trigger, and then froze as he stared in utter disbelief at the familiar features.

It was impossible! He squeezed his eyes shut and then hurriedly opened them again, bringing the rifle up to position. But there was no doubt; the man in the sights of his rifle was the same one who had unwittingly helped him to escape the *Santa Eugenia*; the small fat man with the globular face and the painted hair; the passenger named Dantas—or Dumas or Dortas or something like that!

His jaw tightened; his eyes narrowed. Let God explain to the man when he arrived in heaven the irony of his having aided his own assassin, because regardless of everything else, this man was going to die! The men in the rear seat had risen, preparing to descend. Nacio's lips twisted cruelly; the sight was raised once again, his finger once again began its slow pressure on the trigger.

There was a sudden knock on the door, sharp, peremptory, audible even over the blasting of the television. His head jerked up, startled by the interruption; he stared at the door panel in momentary confusion, dazed by his sudden transformation from the bright sunlight of the Beira Mar to the dim shadows of the room. He waited, his hands locked to the smooth barrel of the gun. Had he actually heard a knock? He had; for it was repeated, once —quickly, as if to give warning—and then there was the sound of a key being inserted in the lock.

His frozen muscles released themselves; with a swift movement he thrust the gun beneath the disheveled bed-

clothes; the armchair was kicked to a less suspicious position in the same movement. The door swung back; a hand
reached in to flick on the overhead light. Nacio came to
his feet, staring in growing fury at the uniformed figure
of an elderly room-maid peering at him through thick
glasses. One stringy arm carried a basket loaded with
bottles and brushes.

Nacio took a step toward her, glowering, his anger even
greater for the relief of knowing the intruder was not
more dangerous. "What do you mean by walking in here
this way? Didn't you see the sign on the door?"

"Sign?" Too late he remembered he had not placed the
sign in position. "I'm sorry, senhor. . . ." She didn't sound
sorry at all; she sounded more accusing. She set her basket
down and marched to the television set, turning its volume
down to a whisper, and then turned to face him. "There
is a sick man just two doors away, senhor. There really is
no need to play the television so loudly."

Nacio clenched his jaws on the outburst that almost
escaped him. This was no time to argue with maids. "All
right; you've turned it down. Now, will you please leave?"

She marched righteously to the door, retrieved her
basket, and then paused, her myopic eyes taking in the
room and its state of disarray. A means of placating her
irritated guest occurred to her. "Would the senhor like me
to straighten up the room, as long as I'm here?"

Nacio silently cursed all hotels, their employees, and
especially interfering room-maids. "I would not like you
to straighten up the room! I would like you to leave and
allow me to be alone!"

She studied him with curiosity that changed to sympathy. "The senhor also does not feel well?"

Good God! What was it with this creature? Couldn't she
understand simple Portuguese? "I feel—" His eyes sud-

denly narrowed; he nodded. "It is true, senhora, I do not feel well. If you will just leave, I shall be able to lie down."

She smiled, pleased by the accuracy of her diagnosis; her thin head bobbed on her neck like some idiot toy. "Then if I at least make up the bed, the senhor will be much more comfortable." She took a step toward the bed; Nacio instantly intercepted her. She attempted to explain. "But, senhor, it will only take a moment."

Nacio gritted his teeth. Words, apparently, were not enough for this stubborn imbecile! He took her by one arm almost roughly, and piloted her toward the door. "I shall be much more comfortable if you do what you are told, and leave!"

She pulled her arm free with a jerk, and sniffed. "I won't be able to straighten up your room until this afternoon, then," she said, making it a dire threat. Nacio clenched his fists; a cold light of viciousness burned in his eyes. The maid seemed to recognize that she had done everything in her power to help, but apparently the senhor did not wish to be helped. With a shrug at the ingratitude of some people, she backed from the room and closed the door behind her.

Nacio savagely jerked it open, slipped the sign on the knob, and almost slammed it shut, turning the lock viciously. He should have put the sign out when Iracema left, but it was just one more thing in the whole ridiculous and needlessly complicated scheme that had been overlooked! He dragged the armchair back into position and brought the gun from beneath the bedclothes. The television would have to remain muted, but that would certainly not save the little man! He brought the gun to his cheek once again and studied the situation at the Memorial.

It took a few seconds for his sight to adjust to the bright sunlight; and then he saw that the ceremony at the Me-

morial had apparently been a short one. The motorcycle
police were already wheeling their vehicles back into the
center of the road, bending forward to touch their sirens.
The television camera truck had pulled to one side, prepared to continue its observation from a different angle.
His telescopic sight found the blue Chrysler; its occupants were climbing in and settling themselves, smiling
and talking. Nacio smiled coldly to himself. Despite all
the interruptions, there was still plenty of time to complete his assignment. He shifted the gun slightly to encompass the black Cadillac behind.

The driver was already in position, his fingers stroking
the steering wheel with professional patience. In the back
seat the man on the near side swung about and sat down,
raised himself slightly to adjust some fold in his jacket, and
then dropped back again. Beyond him the small fat man
was just entering the car, bending forward a bit awkwardly. Nacio's finger was rigid on the trigger; his eye
frozen to the telescope. The little man swung about with
a visible effort, sank down in his seat, and then turned as
if to speak with his companion.

The movement brought his breast pocket into sight.
Nacio's eyes were locked on his target; the gun held rigidly against his cheek might have been a part of him. His
finger slowly, inexorably, pressed the trigger. . . .

Eight

A FEW HOURS EARLIER, on that same bright Tuesday morning, Captain José Da Silva rolled over in his comfortable bed and glowered angrily at the telephone; the instrument, unintimidated, continued its shrill ringing. With a muttered curse for the idiots who had invented the mechanical busybody, he reached over and lifted the receiver, growling into it.

"Yes?"

At the other end of the line, Wilson winced painfully. "Zé, do me a favor—don't scream. Whisper. In fact, whisper quietly. . . ."

Da Silva shoved aside the cover, swinging his feet to the floor, slowly coming awake. He rubbed a large hand across his face to facilitate the process and then yawned. "Wilson? What an hour to call! I didn't get to bed until after two this morning. Now what's the matter?"

"Matter?" Wilson sounded bitter. "Not a thing. Only my head's coming apart at the seams."

A slow smile spread across Da Silva's swarthy features.

"Too much *pinga*? I tried to warn you."

"And I thank you very much. Only you forgot to warn me about mickeys, and that's what they fed me—"

"A mickey? Who? And why?"

Wilson started to nod and then thought better of it; the twinge of pain that shot from his neck to the top of his head almost made him lose his grip on his ice bag. "That's an excellent question. When—and if—I ever recover, I expect to go back there and take that waiter by the scruff of his neck and get an answer to that very question."

Da Silva's grin faded. "What happened?"

"Well," Wilson said, pressing his ice bag tighter against his head and turning from the glaring sunlight at his window, "I went out to this Maloca de Tijuca, parked in the parking lot, and went into the main bar. The place was empty except for one couple—it seems everyone in Rio gets moral on Mondays—and I had a drink and prepared to wait around. And . . ."

"And what?"

Wilson sighed. "And then I had a second drink. And that, it appears, was a major error, because the next thing I knew the room started to get fractious and jump around, and the lights started to get bright, and then they went out. And when I woke up, which was about half an hour ago, I was in my car outside, and the joint was closed. And my head . . ." He shuddered, preferring to try to forget his head.

"So?"

"So how I managed to make it home is going to remain one of the classic mysteries of all times. The *Marie Celeste* pales in comparison. I mention this in case you start getting reports of a dangerous drunk weaving along the Lagôa in an old Chevy."

Da Silva nodded at the telephone in a polite manner, but his thoughts were anything but polite. Where the devil had Freire been? And why hadn't he called in with a report? "I'll remember. And just what would you like us to do about the affair? Send a squad car out to the Maloca and tear the joint apart?"

At the other end of the line Wilson stared at the telephone in amazement. "Do you mean you don't wonder why they would slip a knockout drop to a perfect stranger? It doesn't rouse the slightest curiosity? I know you've been on a sleep diet these past nights, but even so!" He leaned forward, as if in this manner to impress the man at the other end of the connection. "Look, Zé; we know this Nacio used to hang out in this place, and when I go looking for him, I suddenly get taken out of the action." He started to shake his head and then winced. "There has to be a connection."

"Why?" Da Silva asked curiously. "How would Nacio Mendes know who you were, or even what you looked like? When he made his escape, I don't think you were even in Rio yet. Or if you were, I'm sure you two never went around in the same social circles. So why would he go to the trouble of arranging a mickey for you?"

"Do me a favor and don't ask me my own questions." Wilson sounded stiff. "I just asked you why."

"Unless," Da Silva continued thoughtfully, "he did know you, or at least knew who you were. Possibly he had seen you in Washington . . ."

Only the knowledge that any sudden movement would prove painful prevented Wilson from exploding. "Honest to God, Zé! Are you still on that maniac C.I.A. kick?" Heavy sarcasm entered his voice. "And I suppose we hired him when he came begging for a job on his knees, and his method of expressing his gratitude is to feed us all knock-out drops!"

"I wouldn't know," Da Silva said thoughtfully. "I certainly wouldn't rule it out. For example, what action are you suggesting that we take? That we pull a bunch of policemen from their duty guarding the motorcade—all as a result of your unfortunate selection of drinks at the Maloca—and rush out there to waste their time searching the place and putting hot needles under the fingernails of that poor waiter?"

"I wasn't suggesting . . ."

"And have him look at us with innocent baby-blue eyes and tell us that the *pobre Americano* simply couldn't hold his liquor and passed out? And that as an act of compassion —and not to endanger inter-American relations—he put you in your car to sleep it off?"

"And I also suppose," Wilson said, almost gritting his teeth, "that he decided to put the note in my pocket just to keep me warm. Certainly he wouldn't want me to catch cold!"

Da Silva bent back and stared at the telephone. If Wilson's assignment by his superiors in Washington was to confuse either him, or the issues, he was doing it in fine style. "What note?"

"That's one of the things I called to tell you," Wilson said. He sounded a bit smug, as if happy to have finally aroused Da Silva's interest. "When I woke up from that mickey-induced fog, I had this note tucked in my jacket pocket, wrapped around my car keys, where I couldn't miss it. And it simply said: *'Sebastian—here's your watchdog.'* " He took a deep breath, almost of triumph. "And just what do you think of that?"

Da Silva reached over, picked a cigarette from the ever-present package on the nightstand, and lit it. He drew in deeply and blew a wavering cloud of smoke toward the open window. "If you want an honest answer, I don't know what to think of it. One answer, of course, is a romantic triangle. If someone thought you were a private detective who had followed him to the Maloca, then the note makes sense. After all, some people take their own dates to the Maloca, and I hear not all of them are married."

"Except the only people I saw there were a couple who never stopped dancing all the time I was there. And I doubt if they even knew I was there. But just suppose Nacio was there and thought I was trailing him?"

"In that case," Da Silva said slowly, "why would he address the note to someone named Sebastian? Who's Sebastian? Certainly nobody in the police department that I know of." A faint smile crossed his lips; he took a last puff on the cigarette and then crushed it out. "It isn't a common American name, but I have heard it occasionally. Who do you have in your department, or up in Washington, named—"

"Hold it!" At the other end of the line Wilson started to shake his head hopelessly, and then instantly pressed the ice bag against it more tightly. Arguing with Captain José Da Silva was certainly no way to relieve a pounding headache. "Look, Zé, I know you're tired, and I know you've got this crazy idea fixed in your brain—though I'm damned if I know why—but the fact remains I'm telling you the truth. And I'm sure it ties in with this Nacio Mendes."

"On what basis?"

Wilson sighed. "God, you're stubborn! Forget it; I was just trying to be helpful. As soon as the four aspirin I took begin to work, I'll come down to your office." The sarcasm returned to his voice. "I don't suppose you'd mind terribly if we compare the handwriting on this note with any samples you might have in your folder of this Nacio's handwriting, would you?"

"Not at all," Da Silva said magnanimously. "Be my guest."

"My, you're sweet when you get up in the morning!" Wilson said bitterly, and hung up.

Da Silva frowned at the telephone a moment, his eyes narrowing, and then depressed the button. He released it and began to dial. The operator at central police took his call, transferred it to the proper extension, and began to ring. The telephone was lifted instantly; a bright and wide-awake voice answered.

"Lieutenant Perreira—"

"Perreira, this is Da Silva. How are things going?"

"All right, Captain. Everyone's on the job, and for a change half of them didn't report in sick. The motorcade is scheduled to start in about an hour, and all of our people are in place."

"Good," Da Silva said, and meant it. "And how about the reports on last night's check-up?"

"Most of them are in, on your desk. Sergeant Ramos is writing his up now. He ought to be done pretty soon." His voice remained cheerful, the result of having gotten a full eight hours sleep the night before. "I went through them. Nothing out of the way."

"That's good. I'll be down as soon as I get dressed. And there's one more thing— Why didn't Freire report in?"

"Didn't he call you? I assumed when he didn't report to me that he was reporting directly to you. I'll . . . Pardon me a moment, Captain . . ." There followed a few minutes of silence as Perreira spoke with someone in the office; when he came back on the line the light cheerfulness was gone, replaced by a savage anger. "Captain, we just got a report. Some kids playing out on the beach at Tijuca found a man's body. They told a cop and he checked it out. It's Freire."

"*What!*"

"The body was about a hundred yards up the beach from the Maloca de Tijuca, if you know the place. He was shot. Just once." The first burst of anger in his voice had been replaced by the cold official tones of a lieutenant reporting a crime to his superior. "Do you want us to pick up the man he was following? That American, Wilson?"

"No," Da Silva said. "I just finished speaking with Wilson. He didn't know he was being followed, and anyway it isn't necessary. I'm sure he didn't have anything to do with it, and in any event he's coming down to headquarters in a little while." He took a deep breath, staring at the telephone, a harsh light in his dark eyes. So Wilson had somehow managed to stir up a hornet's nest, even if he wasn't aware of it. And as a result a good man was dead. He leaned forward. "Perreira, how many bad boys do we have around named Sebastian?"

Perreira accepted what seemed to be a change in subject without surprise; he knew Captain Da Silva and knew he never wasted his questions. "Sebastian what?"

Da Silva frowned at the telephone. Apparently too much sleep was as bad as not enough sleep for clogging the brain. "If I knew his last name I wouldn't be asking you. I don't know his last name. Just Sebastian."

Perreira shook his head. "Just Sebastian, Captain? That's a fairly common name. My guess would be quite a few. Is there anything else you can give me? A bad boy in what respect?"

"A very bad boy." Da Silva studied the wall opposite him

without seeing it. "He might have had something to do with Nacio Mendes, maybe sometime in the past, although I don't recall that name anywhere in his dossier."

"I saw the notice on Mendes," Perreira said, and then sat up. "Do you think he could have been responsible for—?"

"I'm not thinking anything," Da Silva said shortly. "I'm just trying to fit a man named Sebastian into the picture. He may be somebody who has some connection with killing in general—killing for profit, that is. Or he might have . . ." He paused. Or he might have what? A record for spitting on sidewalks, or parking in illegal zones such as the unloading dock for catering trucks at Santos Dumont? He rubbed his face wearily. "I don't know. All I know is the name Sebastian."

"I'll check it out." Perreira didn't sound too sanguine.

"I wish you would. Or, wait a minute!" Da Silva leaned forward, frowning down at the rug. "What about Sebastian Pinheiro? Whatever happened to him? He was tied into a few killings."

"Pinheiro? I haven't heard of him for years. And there never was anything to tie him to Mendes that we could ever find. As a matter of fact," Perreira added bitterly, "there was very little to tie him to anyone. He was a real cute one. We never did get a conviction, though I'm damned sure he arranged at least four killings I know of, and God knows how many I don't know of."

"True."

"And anyway," Perreira added thoughtfully, "I seem to remember a notice from Immigration about him. He left the country a few months ago; went to Argentina, as I recall. There wasn't any basis for stopping him from traveling, but they still keep us informed."

"But did he come back?"

"I don't know. I'll have to check."

"Do that," Da Silva said. "And also check on any other stray Sebastians that might fit the bill."

"Right, Captain." Perreira paused a moment. "And how about the Freire deal?"

Da Silva grimaced. "The usual, I suppose. Damn, I wish we weren't tied up so much with this blasted O.A.S. thing! Although," he added slowly, "I have a feeling that Freire's murder was somehow part of it."

"And you think this man Sebastian was somehow connected with it, Captain?"

"Yes," Da Silva said, and was surprised to hear the word fall from his own lips. "Yes, I do."

"Then in that case," Perreira said with a coldness that was almost ferocious, "we'll dig him out if we have to unearth every Sebastian this side of hell!" He seemed to realize suddenly that he had been bordering on the dramatic. "I'd better get right to it. Is there anything else, Captain?"

"That's it," Da Silva said, and hung up.

He got to his feet, beginning to shed his pajamas. Perreira was a good man, and if there was anything to be dug up on this new name, Sebastian, he would dig it out. If the name means anything as far as this case is concerned, he added sourly to himself; if Wilson isn't just leading me around by my nose. He shook his head wearily. And, of course, if it isn't too late as far as the O.A.S. meetings are concerned, even if it does mean something. . . .

Captain Da Silva stuck his head in at the door to Lieutenant Perreira's tiny office; his subordinate's desk was unoccupied. Sergeant Ramos, wedged in the small space between the desk and the window, and sweating over his report, looked up gratefully. Any interruption in the laborious task of putting his thoughts to paper was always welcome. The thin ball-point pen he grasped was almost swallowed by his huge fist; he laid it aside and smiled at his superior.

"The lieutenant isn't here, Captain. I think he's trying to get some information for you."

"All right. Tell him I'll be in my office."

"Sure. And Captain, how about that Freire deal?" The big man shook his head. "Rough, huh?"

"Real rough," Da Silva said.

"It sure was. And Captain"—the sergeant dismissed the problem of his murdered co-worker in consideration of his own—"I could tell you what happened a lot easier than writing it."

Da Silva's thick finger aimed pointedly and positively at the pad on the table before Ramos; he closed the door behind him and walked down the hall to his own office. His elderly secretary automatically began to smile at him as he entered, and then wiped it off instantly in remembrance that a man in their department had been killed in the line of duty that day. He nodded and walked into his inner sanctum, hung his jacket on the back of his chair, and then slipped out of his revolver harness, laying it on the corner of his desk. He dropped into a chair and rubbed his shoulder. In the growing heat of the day a wide band of perspiration already showed where the leather straps had passed.

The artist's sketches of Nacio Mendes were lying in the center of the desk blotter, where they had been returned after being reproduced. He shoved them brusquely to one side and reached for his intercom box, drawing it closer, pressing buttons to bring it to life and to give him the proper connection. When it began to sputter scratchily, he considered it ready.

"Captain Da Silva here. I want to be tied into the system."

"All of it, Captain?"

"No, just the Radio Patrulha at the O.A.S. parade. And tie me into the microphone, also."

"Right, Captain."

The small box hummed statically, scratching and rising and fading. Da Silva adjusted a small knob and leaned forward. "Hello? Hello? What's the matter with this damned thing?"

A voice came back, tinny and distorted by the apparatus. *"Sim? Quem fala?"*

"This is Captain Da Silva here. How are things going?"

"Fine, Captain. We're just getting started now. From the Gloria." Even over the deficiencies of the speaker system the next words came out sadder and more somber. "That was a terrible thing that happened to Freire, wasn't it, Captain?"

"It was," Da Silva said shortly and glowered at the box wondering why bad news always seemed to get around faster than good. "Where is your patrol car located?"

"About halfway down the line. There're four cars ahead of us, not counting the television truck, and five more behind us. And six motorcycles in the escort in front of the motorcade and four more in the rear. And men along the way in the crowd, of course, plus the military police along the barriers."

Which is about as much as one can do, Da Silva thought. "Is there much of a crowd?"

"Quite a few." The disembodied voice sounded almost admiring, pleased with the audience, and then it fell slightly. "Nothing like we had when the *fûtebol* team came back from winning the World Cup, but plenty."

"All right," Da Silva said evenly. "You keep on in a normal way. I'll be tuned in from here."

"Right, Captain."

The swarthy captain leaned forward, tuning the volume down to a less raucous screech, just as Perreira came through the doorway. Da Silva glanced up inquiringly; the young lieutenant shook his head.

"Nothing of interest, Captain. Not as far as people named Sebastian are concerned. Rape, yes; robbery, more than yes. In fact, you name the crime and we've got a criminal named Sebastian to match. But killing for profit?" The lieutenant shook his head. "It's amazing how few people named Sebastian have gotten into trouble for that reason lately."

"A pity," Da Silva said dryly, and then looked at his subordinate with a sharper eye. "How about Pinheiro?"

Perreira glanced at the paper in his hand and then shrugged. "He's back in this country, but there's nothing to tie him to anybody. Or anything. He came in from Portugal by KLM about a month ago."

"From Portugal?" Da Silva sat up, frowning. "You said he'd gone to Argentina!"

"He did. And from Argentina to Portugal. And from Portugal back home. Why?"

"Because Mendes came from Portugal, too." Da Silva stared at the other a moment, his brow wrinkled. "Do you have any address for Pinheiro?"

"Just an old one," Perreira said. "He used to live at the top of the Ladeira Portofino, off of the Rua Riachuelo. In Lapa. I've got the number here." He shrugged and stared down at the slip in his hand. "It used to be Number Sixty-Nine, but he could have moved since then. We never got a conviction on the man, so he doesn't have to report any changes to us."

Da Silva started to mark it down when there was a tap on the door and Sergeant Ramos poked his head in. When neither of the occupants instructed him to leave, he properly construed it as permission to enter and shoved his huge bulk into the room. The wrinkled state of the sheaf of papers in his hand clearly showed the ordeal he had suffered in writing his report.

"Here's that report, Captain. It doesn't say much, because there wasn't much to say." He bent forward to drop the papers on the desk and then paused. "Hey! What's Lover Boy's picture doing here? What was he picked up for? Cohabiting?" A grin crossed his normally expressionless face. "Not that I blame him, with that dame."

Da Silva frowned up at him. "What?"

"Him." Ramos' thick thumb stabbed in the direction of Nacio's picture; the thin mustached face on the ink sketch seemed to stare back bitterly, as if accusing the sergeant of being a stool pigeon.

Da Silva sat up, electrified. *"What! You've seen him?"*

"Sure." Ramos was surprised at the vehemence of his superior; he turned to Perreira to find the lieutenant staring at him with equal tenseness. "Up in Room 825 at the Serrador. Doctor Carabello. And his girl friend. It's all in the report—"

Da Silva had come to his feet even as the other was speaking; he reached for his holster and his jacket in the same move. "Perreira, get a car! And—" He paused a moment. "Or better yet—" He bent forward, turning up the volume on the intercom. "Radio Patrulha?"

The thin metallic voice came on. *"Sim?"*

"How quick can you get over to the Serrador Hotel? Room 825. I want to detain anyone you find there!"

"I don't know, Captain." The voice was doubtful. "We're stopped here now for some ceremony at the War

Memorial, but we'd have to go all the way to the end of the Beira Mar to get off. The crowds are solid both sides. Unless—"

The voice broke off a moment, replaced by a flurry of scratchy static; when it resumed it was high and shrill, overwhelmed by the importance of events, its excitement communicating itself even over the inadequacies of the apparatus.

"Captain! Something's happening up ahead! I think near the War Memorial!"

"*What!*" Da Silva bent closer, his eyes blazing. "What happened?"

"I don't know. The motorcycle escort pulled away, and then the first car, but when the second car started up it pulled over; damned near hit the steps! I think there was an accident or something! The whole crowd is closing in!"

Da Silva exploded. "Well, damn it, don't sit there! I want to know what happened! And to whom!"

"I'll get right over there. . . ."

"And thank you very much," Da Silva growled, and glared at the small box. Perreira was already on his feet, standing near the door.

"I'll get over to the Serrador, Captain. We'll cover the streets all around the place."

Da Silva held up his hand almost wearily. "Hold it. We don't even know what happened. And if it's what we both think, it's too late now, anyway. We couldn't possibly cover that maze of streets before he'd be away from there." He swung back to the intercom, clamping his jaws to prevent his blasting into the small box. "Well? Well?"

A new voice answered him, deeply apologetic. "The sergeant's on his way over there on foot, Captain. The car couldn't possibly get through. The crowds are all

around the car up there. The motorcycle police are trying
to clear a space for the ambulance now—"

"What ambulance? Damn it, what happened?"

"I don't know, Captain. . . . "

Da Silva opened his mouth and then slowly closed it
again. Blasting at the man in the Radio Patrulha certainly
wouldn't help anything. He looked up at Perreira.

"Unless we want to wait here all day for news, we're
going to have to assume that whatever happened down
there involved Nacio Mendes, and that he's tied in with
Sebastian Pinheiro somehow."

"On what basis, Captain?"

"On the basis that we don't have anything else," Da
Silva said bitterly. He frowned at the man above him.
"Where does this Pinheiro live again?"

"I told you, Captain. On the top of the Ladeira Portofino, number sixty-nine." Perreira shook his head doubtfully. "But that was over three years ago."

"Then let's just hope the housing shortage kept him
there," Da Silva said shortly. His thick fingers drummed
on the desk. "That's pretty open up there, isn't it?"

Perreira understood him. "Up to the top it's open.
After that, of course, it's all woods." He studied his superior. "From the house you'd be able to see anyone coming up the ladeira."

"And beyond it? Doesn't it lead up the mountain?"

"That's true." Perreira thought a moment. "You could
take a car up to Santa Tereza and leave it there, and then
come down through the *matto*. But it would take a lot
longer to get there that way."

Da Silva frowned at the map on the wall a moment and
then made up his mind. His dark eyes came up to meet
those of his young lieutenant. "All right. You take two
men and go up to Santa Tereza, and then come down from

above. I'll take Ramos, here, and go up the ladeira from Lapa." A sudden thought came to him. "Wait a second —how about the backs of the houses along the ladeira?"

Perreira shook his head decisively. "Those houses are all built right up against the rock, Captain. It would be almost impossible to try to go up that way."

"Or to go down," Da Silva said slowly, and nodded in satisfaction. "All right; you get up there and cover the house from the top, from the woods. We'll come up the front."

Perreira looked unhappy. "You'll be a sitting duck on those steps, Captain, if there's any trouble . . ." One look at the expression that flashed across Da Silva's swarthy face and he swallowed the balance of his words. "Yes sir!"

"How long will it take you to get up there and get set?"

"From here, about forty-five minutes to an hour."

"Then we'll make it in an hour and fifteen minutes." He checked his watch. "It's ten thirty-five now. At eleven-fifty." His jaw tightened. "We'll drop in for lunch."

"Yes, sir," Perreira said, and closed the door behind himself.

Da Silva bent forward, twisting the knob of the intercom; his only reward was an increase in static. "Hello? Hello? What the hell's the matter with this thing?"

"*Sim?*"

"Damn it! What's the matter with you men down there? Are you tongue-tied or something? What's happening down there?"

The voice of the other tried to appeal to the captain's logic. "The sergeant isn't back yet—"

"Great!" Da Silva said in disgust. "I'll read about it in tomorrow's newspaper!" He came to his feet, reaching for his holster, slipping it on. The telephone rang as he took his jacket from behind the chair; he picked it up, barking into it. "Yes?"

It was his secretary from the outer office. "An outside telephone call for you, Captain."

"I'll call them later," Da Silva said brusquely, and prepared to hang up.

"But it's from Buenos Aires—"

"Oh!" He tossed his jacket to one side and dropped back into his chair, dragging the instrument closer. "Hello? All right, I'll wait." His hand brought a pad closer and dug a pencil from a drawer while operators traded weird sounds in his ear. At last the line cleared and he leaned forward, his eyes bright.

"Hello? Echavarria? What?" He began to scribble furiously, nodding at the telephone. "What? Oh, good! Very good! The ship was already there? And you saw the captain? What? Good—very good. . . . And the note? It was? You're sure? Wonderful! What? Yes, I've got it." He finished writing and nodded to the far-off voice, his fingers twiddling the pencil. "Yes, I've got it. But you're really sure about the note?"

The faint buzz of the voice as heard in the quiet room seemed to increase in intensity; Da Silva nodded again. "Fine. In fact, more than fine. If you're satisfied, I am. What?" A faint smile came across his tired face. "Of course I'm lucky. It's better than having brains any time. Right. And thanks a million. I'll be in touch."

He placed the instrument back on the hook and then stared at it for several moments, letting the last pieces of the puzzle drop neatly into their proper slots. Now, if Sebastian had only not moved his residence—and if, of course, he was the proper Sebastian—and if . . . A lot of ifs, he thought to himself, but on the other hand the thing made sense, and that's what answered the motives of men. The scribbled notes were folded and tucked into his shirt pocket. He came to his feet and reached for his jacket, tilting his head in the direction of the door; Ramos, who had been standing quietly to one side, only vaguely understanding what was going on, instantly understood the gesture. He nodded and opened the door for his chief; on the outside, with one hand poised to knock, stood Wilson.

The nondescript man lowered his hand almost apologetically and looked from Ramos to Da Silva.

"Hello, Sergeant. Hello, Zé. What's all the excitement? I saw Perreira when I came in, and he looked like he was on his way to a fire. And you two look like you're on your way to hold the ladder for him." He reached into a pocket and brought out a piece of paper. "Here's that note I was telling you about, Zé."

Da Silva finished slipping into his jacket, took the note and glanced at it, and then tossed it on the desk. "I'm afraid it'll have to wait. We're on our way—"

"Wait?" Wilson frowned. "You mean you're not even going to check the handwriting?"

"No." Da Silva smiled faintly. "I've got a theory, and if your note wasn't written by Mendes, I'd have to throw it away. And right now there isn't time for that." He studied Wilson's drawn face a moment. "You know, Wilson, you were in on this thing right from the beginning—in fact, you and your story about the man who disappeared from the ambulance were really the start of this case. So how would you like to be in on the ending?" He took a deep breath. "I hope. . . ."

Wilson studied him suspiciously. "What's up?"

"Come on along and find out." Da Silva took him by the arm and urged him in the direction of the door. "You may find it interesting."

For a moment Wilson held back, and then allowed himself to be drawn toward the door. "Well, all right," he said a bit doubtfully. "There's just one thing, though . . ."

Da Silva stared at him. "And what's that?"

"Well," Wilson said, putting his hand to his head and wincing slightly, "if you're going in a police car and feel like using the siren, do me a favor and play it softly. . . ."

Nine

NACIO MADEIRA MENDES, slowly
climbing the Ladeira Portofino, reviewed for the fourth
or fifth time the steps he had taken once he had seen the
small figure in the black Cadillac slam back against the
side of the car, and had seen the look of incredulous
shock flash across the small round face. There had been
no time for further observation, nor had any been re-
quired. Nacio's mind had coldly blanked out the frozen
tableau caught in the tubular gunsight, and had turned
instantly to the steps now necessary to be taken. Nor had
his recollection of those steps uncovered any error or over-
sight.

The gun had been thrust deep beneath the bedclothes
and a pillow tossed on top to disguise its outline; the
armchair had been swung to a new position. His eyeglasses had been hooked into place, his revolver recov-
ered from the dresser and tucked beneath his belt and
his jacket buttoned over it; the doorknob of the room
had been properly wiped when he left. All according to

schedule. He even recalled with a touch of amusement the head poked inquiringly out of a door near his when he emerged, a head seeking the source of the strange noise; without breaking his stride he had pointed farther along the dim hallway and then had reached the stairway exit and was trotting down the steep concrete steps. The corridor below led to the employees' entrance, and he had paused in the shadowed hall to strip his gloves from his hands and shove them deep into one pocket, and had then pressed with his shoulder against the heavy locking-bar, stepping out into the street.

The growing sound of a siren coming along the Beira Mar had echoed in the distance, no very unusual sound in Rio, identifying an ambulance he was certain would be of no use to his victim. He could picture the growing excitement and startled disbelief of the spectators stirring across the Praça Paris before the War Memorial, but here in the narrow Rua Senador Dantas no knowledge of the event had had time to penetrate. Nor had there been any further indication of the fateful event as he had calmly walked to the Lapa arches, marched beneath them into the Rua Riachuelo, and had eventually come to the Ladeira Portofino.

He paused a moment on the ladeira, relaxing, leaning against the low stone railing that edged the steep stairs, staring off into the distance over the red roofs below. Eight days before, he had climbed those steps for the first time in over three years; cold, wet, uncomfortable, uncertain as to his future or the wisdom of having returned to Rio at that time or under those circumstances. Now, in the bright sunlight and the warm breeze, he was mounting them again, but this time with all doubts resolved. Now a job had been successfully accomplished, and a fee was waiting to be collected, a fee beyond anything he had ever dreamed of earning. Plans would have to be made for removing himself from the city as quickly as was consistent with proper safety, but for the moment these plans could wait. For the moment there was triumph to be savored and money to be counted, and if there was enough money to be shared with Sebastian, then there was also enough triumph to be shared as well. No harm could come from admitting to Sebastian that the scheme, which he had never liked too well, had indeed been quite good. Or at least, he added to himself, it had worked, and that was the only thing that counted.

He resumed his climb, taking his time, approaching the top of the stairs, anticipating the smile of welcome on Sebastian's face, a smile he realized would be mostly self-congratulatory for having engineered the complicated plan, but a welcoming smile nonetheless. Even Iracema would be forced to demonstrate some sign of admiration. His eyes came up as he turned into the small areaway fronting the paneled door; a curtain dropped on one of the first-floor windows, swaying back into place. This time, it appeared he would not be kept waiting.

Nor was he. Even as he reached for the doorbell the door swung open in his face, but the welcoming smile he had anticipated from Sebastian was oddly missing. In its place was a frown so fierce, a glare so out of character for the large fleshy man, that for a moment a slight chill struck the smaller man. What on earth could be the matter with Sebastian? What could possibly have caused this reception? And then the explanation struck him. Of course! The murder of the police officer at the Maloca de Tijuca had undoubtedly hit the newspapers and the radio, and Sebastian would have known by now of his presence there the previous evening. So what! He shoved himself past the larger man, swaggering into the dim room. On the arm of a chair Iracema sat, her head turned down, her hair shadowing her face, her eyes staring at the rug. Nacio shook his head. Amateurs, he thought with an inner sneer; beginners! Did they honestly think the killing of the police officer more important that the successful assassination he had accomplished just a short while before? Or that he was so careless as to have left anything at either killing to lead to himself, or through him, to them?

He shrugged and swaggered into the room farther; the girl came to her feet and moved to the window, as if to keep a distance between them. Nacio smiled faintly. "How about a drink?"

Sebastian stared at him a moment as if in disbelief. When he spoke it was in a half-whisper, his voice almost barren of any emotion. "You fool . . . You incompetent idiot . . ."

Nacio looked up, his eyes narrowing, his thin lips tightening. Talk like this from anyone, but especially from a fat coward like Sebastian, was far from common. He bit back his temper, forcing himself to relax. Success had crowned the more important killing, and if Sebastian was irritated with the other, it was just too bad. There was no need to see each other ever again after today, and the fat man could stew in his memories.

"What did you say?"

"I said you were an incompetent idiot! An imbecile! That I had to go all the way to Lisbon to find!" The repetition of the insults seemed to have strengthened the deep voice; the large hands clenched and unclenched in anger.

Nacio stared at him a moment and then shrugged carelessly. "Those are pretty strong words, my friend."

"Strong words?" Sebastian's eyes widened at the other's

attitude; he almost sputtered. *"Strong words?"* His voice rasped in his throat as if speech were painful. "Three months in planning this thing—three months? More! Every last detail! And over five thousand conto spent in expenses—" His voice grew even more bitter. "Idiot things, like buying you a fake passport, and those fancy clothes you're wearing. And you call it strong words when I don't congratulate you for blowing the whole thing?" His large body leaned forward a bit; he seemed to be holding in an explosion with an almost superhuman effort.

"Blowing what thing?" Nacio suddenly laughed; the whole thing was too absurd. So it wasn't the affair of the police officer that was bothering Sebastian after all; the poor stupid fat slob somehow seemed to have the crazy idea that he had missed his target! What foolishness! "What are you talking about?"

Sebastian gritted his teeth, hissing through them. "I'm talking about a radio announcement that came through less than five minutes ago, saying that despite an attack that had just been made upon him, Juan Dorcas of Argentina expects to address the opening session of the O.A.S. tomorrow morning! That's what I'm talking about!"

Nacio's laughter died instantly, replaced by an icy calm. He seemed to shrink into himself; the wary instinct of an animal defending himself against a threat suspected but not confirmed. "You're crazy!"

"Am I?" A big thumb jerked angrily toward one corner of the room. "Am I? Would you like to hear it for yourself? There's the radio over there; tune it in. Listen for yourself. It's all they're talking about; it's on every station."

"It's impossible! I saw him when the bullet hit him!" Nacio's eyes suddenly narrowed; his jaw clenched. So

Sebastian was still trying to play games! "What are you trying to pull?"

"What am I—?" Words failed the larger man. "What am I—?"

"That's right. I did the job and I want my money. And I want it right now!" Nacio's hand crept toward his belt; his eyes were points of ice in his lean face. "So get it!"

"Get it? Get what?" Sebastian stared at him. "You want to be paid for costing me a fortune? For throwing away what I planned on so long and so carefully?"

The revolver suddenly appeared in Nacio's hand. The time to end this charade had arrived; his surprise that Sebastian would attempt to pull something like this was tempered by the knowledge that no man could be trusted forever, and particularly not where a sum this size was involved. His voice hardened.

"You heard me. I want that money."

Sebastian faced him, frozen, his widened eyes riveted on the revolver. "Where did you get that gun?"

"In a bag of popcorn! Come on! I did my part of the job and I intend to be paid for it."

"Put down that gun—"

"I'll put it down when I've been paid. Come on! I'm sure the money's here in the house!"

At the window Iracema suddenly spoke. Her voice was dull, almost uninterested, as if the disappointment of the day had drained away the last of the vitality that had kept her going for the past week. "There are some men coming up the ladeira. . . . Strangers. . . ."

Nacio almost sneered at the pitiful attempt to draw his attention. Strangers never came to the top of the ladeira. Across from him Sebastian took a tentative step toward a table in one corner. The gun came up swiftly, rigidly.

"Stay where you are! Move away from that table!"

"They're still coming," Iracema said quietly, almost conversationally.

The disinterest, almost boredom, of her voice caused Nacio to waver a moment. He stepped quickly backward, toward the window, sweeping the girl aside with a stiff arm. The revolver came up, checking the larger man in place, before he chanced a quick glance about the edge of the curtain. There *were* men coming up the ladeira! Still, there was no reason to suspect they had anything to do with either him or Sebastian, or the house; there were other houses on the Portofino. But still, there was no doubt it was rare.

A frown appeared on his old-young face; he took a second glance, studying the men below with greater care, and then froze in rigid anger. One of the men he recognized; the watchdog Sebastian had set on him the night before at the Maloca! He swung back, his face white with fury.

"So that was the idea, eh? I pull the job and then you have some of your boys take care of me, eh? So you keep the whole bundle. Well, if they take me, you won't be around to watch!"

Sebastian took a step forward, staring at him as if he were mad. "What are you talking about?"

"I'm talking about this," Nacio said quietly through clenched teeth. He raised the revolver and calmly pulled the trigger. The explosion rocked the room, mingled with the sudden terrified scream of the girl. The large man staggered back under the force of the bullet; his hands came up, fingers curled like talons, and then he lurched forward toward his assailant. The second bullet tore through his neck, swinging him about sharply; his hands groped blindly at the spurting blood, as if trying to hold life within him by sheer force, and then he crashed to the floor.

A whirlwind of thrashing arms and legs struck Nacio, driving him to his knees before he knew what had happened. He tried to twist loose, to bring up the gun again, but an infuriated Iracema was swarming over him, clawing at him madly with sharpened fingernails, her full body used to press him down; her breath was hot and sweet on his face. Her hands locked on the gun, tearing it brutally from his grasp. An almost insane continuous crooning came from her throat, more frightening than any sound Nacio could remember. With a supreme effort bordering on panic he thrashed about and finally managed to break the hold and squirm loose, coming to his feet in a wild stagger to make for the door.

The three men trudging warily up the long granite stairway, paused at the sharp flat cracks of the pistol shots, echoing in the narrow defile and resounding from the mountain above. Da Silva was the first to recover. He started up the remaining stone slabs at a run, his eyes bright, his revolver out and gripped tightly in his large hand. Behind him Wilson and Ramos clambered up the steep steps, panting, their eyes locked on the small house at the top.

The door they were watching as they climbed was suddenly torn open; a disheveled figure appeared there, head jerking wildly from side to side in search of escape. The small spectacled man outlined against the black of the open doorway took the two steps necessary to reach the edge of the ladeira and then swung about, preparing to make a dash for the protection of the wooded *serra* above. Da Silva brought his gun up, shouting, but in that moment there were a series of sharp explosions from within the house. The figure jerked, twisted as if uncertain, and then slowly turned in a grotesque pirouette. It took a hesitant step, and then another, paused at the edge of the top step a moment as if considering the extensive view, tottered, crumpled, and came hurtling down the ladeira toward the three men pressed back in frozen shock against the low stone railing. It landed above them, bounced flaccidly twice, and came to a final rest against the wall, hands flung outward as if in supplication, face crushed cruelly into the crevice formed by the step and the rough stone wall. A small trail of blood instantly stained the pale stone, running from the hidden smashed face to trickle delicately to the step below.

Da Silva took the two steps to reach the body in a leap, bending down instantly to examine it; Wilson paused at his side, crouching, breathing heavily, one hand going automatically to his forehead to ease the pounding pain there. Sergeant Ramos went on up past his chief without awaiting instruction, bending low to take what little protection the short wall offered, jumping from step to step. There was a cry from the woods beyond the house and Lieutenant Perreira came running down from the green cover of the *matto,* followed by another man. They dashed across the open space, dodging from side to side, and then paused at the wall of the house, edging cautiously toward the corner.

Da Silva rolled the body over; it seemed to resist a moment as if resenting the invasion of its privacy, and then came heavily, arms flopping wide, slapping down at the stone step. The eyeglasses had smashed and were white circles of powdered glass skewed on the bloody face. Da Silva bent over distastefully and stripped them away. The unseeing eyes stared back at him; the thin lips dribbling blood were drawn back from the broken teeth. Da Silva made a small grimace of repugnance.

"It's Nacio Mendes, all right. . . ."

There was a shout from the house above; Ramos was standing in the open doorway, tucking his gun into his holster, waving him to come up. Perreira and his companion had disappeared within the house. Da Silva straightened up slowly, replaced his gun in its holster, and then with a shake of his head stared up at the house.

"Let's go."

The dim shadows of the room, after the brilliant sunshine outside, caused the two men to pause as they entered, waiting until their sight had adjusted to the semi-twilight within. The sharp odor of cordite filled the room; wisps of smoke still eddied in the still air. The other three detectives were standing hesitantly to one side, their expressions an odd combination of professional interest in the dead man sprawled on the floor, and a certain sympathetic respect for the girl sitting beside it, cradling the bloody head in her lap. She made no sound at all, but merely continued to brush the wavy hair with her hand, stroking it gently, rocking back and forth in silent grief. Da Silva studied the dim room a moment and then walked over to a chair and picked up a small briefcase resting there; he opened it, stared into its empty depths, and then studied the manufacturer's name impressed on the inside of the cover. He laid it aside, glancing at Perreira; the lieutenant nodded as he tipped his head toward the body.

"It's Pinheiro, all right." His voice was restrained, as if in respect for the girl's wordless sorrow.

Da Silva nodded. He made his voice brisk, businesslike, in order to break the spell the scene was casting on its viewers. "All right. Let's get her away from here. I'll talk to her later at headquarters." He frowned down at the spread-eagled figure. "And cover him up with something. And also cover the one down on the ladeira as well, until the wagon comes. The kids around this neighborhood see enough without having to see that."

"Yes, sir." Perreira muttered an instruction to his assistant and then bent to take the girl by the hand. She rose quietly, almost majestically, stared down at the dead body a moment, and then docilely followed Perreira to the doorway, unconsciously wiping her bloody hands against her thighs. The other detective took a serape from the couch and draped it as best he could over the dead man, and then followed the lieutenant to the door. Ramos picked up a small throw rug and also left the room, going down the steep ladeira toward the body wedged on the stone step.

Wilson, watching the scene from one side, stared down a moment at the shapeless mound on the floor and then raised startled eyes to Da Silva's rigid face.

"My God! What on earth happened?"

"A disagreement," Da Silva said dryly, and slowly shook his head. "An apparent difference of opinion. In which both lost." He looked up. "It seems fairly clear that the girl shot Mendes, and most probably because Mendes shot Pinheiro. Why?" He shrugged humorlessly. "Maybe we'll find out from the girl down at the Delegacia. And maybe not. I can't really see it as being too important. Neither one of them will be missed."

"And who is Pinheiro?"

Da Silva glanced at him curiously. "I keep forgetting you don't know. He's the Sebastian you wanted me to look for so desperately. Well, we managed to find him." His eyes dropped to contemplate the body on the floor broodingly. "If you still want him, you can have him."

Wilson squeezed his eyes shut a moment against the pain that was returning to split his head, and then opened them. "The man in the note, I gather. But who, exactly, is he?"

"Pinheiro?" Da Silva shrugged. "He is—or was, rather a middleman in arranging for people to be killed. A go-between. A one-man employment agency with enough contacts on both sides of the law to bring both a murderer and a victim together. A marriage-broker, in reverse. Who hired one assassin too many." He brought his eyes up from the lump on the floor. "He is—or was—the one who arranged for Nacio Mendes to come back to Brazil."

"But why?"

Da Silva stared at him. "Why? To kill Juan Dorcas, of course."

Wilson shook his head impatiently and instantly regretted it. He waited until the pounding had subsided. "I don't mean that, I mean, for whom? Who paid for the job?"

A faint smile touched the corners of Da Silva's lips, a smile that did not extend to his brooding eyes. He studied Wilson's pale face a moment, and then picked up the briefcase that had interested him before. "That's right; you really don't know, do you? Well, I don't think this is a time for secrets. This was apparently used to bring the payoff, and the money isn't here. And it has a Buenos Aires manufacturer's name. So . . ."

He walked to the foot of the stairway leading above and called up it softly. In the quiet room his voice echoed clearly to the floor above, emotionless and steady.

"Senhor?" There was complete silence in the small house; in the distance the faint echo of a dying siren seemed to give an almost false touch of drama to the scene. Da Silva took a deep breath. "Senhor? I'm sure you hear me. I think you'd better come down now. I know

you're up there, and I think there has been enough killing for one morning. . . ."

Wilson was staring at him in surprise, as if the events
of the past few moments had driven his tall Brazilian
friend out of his mind. "Zé! What on earth—?"

Da Silva raised a hand sharply for silence without taking
his eyes from the stairway. He stepped a bit closer to the
foot of the stairs, calling again. His voice remained soft,
but there was steel in the steady tones.

"Senhor? I know you're there. If I am forced to come
up and get you—"

There was silence for a moment, and then the hesitant
scrape of a foot on the landing above. A man appeared on
the steps, placing one neatly shod foot before him slowly,
carefully, almost daintily descending. Da Silva moved to
one side, twisting the switch of a lamp, his revolver rigidly held before him. In the cone of light that sprang up
in the dim room the small body came into view a bit at
a time. First the tiny feet in their highly polished shoes,
then the short legs, then the round stomach and the arms
held with his fists clenched tightly at his side, and finally
the full fat face with the hairline mustache and the hair
that seemed to be painted in place. He reached the bottom of the steps and stood quietly, watchfully, staring
at the two men before him with wide liquid eyes.

Wilson turned to Da Silva, frowning in amazement.
"And who the devil is this?"

"This?" Da Silva was considering the little man with
almost clinical detachment. "This is a hungry, vicious,
ungrateful little monster with large ambitions. Who might
have gotten away with it if he hadn't tried to be cuter than
he is. And who caused the death of three men, one of
whom worked for me and will be missed. . . ."

The small man opened his mouth as if to say something and then closed it, locking his jaw. The large swarthy man before him was frightening in his very lack of emotion. The fat face was pallid; beads of sweat began to form on his broad forehead. Wilson stared from the perspiring face to Da Silva's narrowed eyes and stony expression.

"But, who—?"

"You want an introduction? Of course." Da Silva turned to the small pale man and tipped his head slightly in a grotesque parody of politeness. "This is Senhor Wilson, of the American Embassy, and a very close friend of mine." His head moved, contemplating Wilson.

"And this animal"—his voice remained the same— "is Senhor Alvinor Dorcas, brother of Juan Dorcas, but unfortunately for him and his plans, not at the moment his brother's heir. . . ."

Ten

WILSON watched his friend Captain José Da Silva push his way through the crowded tables of the Santos Dumont restaurant; he leaned over and poured a glass of cognac to the brim, and then carefully placed it across the table in position for ready consumption. Da Silva, arriving, removed his jacket with a profound sigh of relief, draped it over the back of his chair, and dropped into his seat. He noticed the glass before him and reached for it gratefully. Wilson frowned.

"You might at least say hello first."

Da Silva paused with the glass halfway to his lips. "Hello." He finished the drink, wiped his lips, and shook his head reproachfully. "And never interrupt a man in the midst of a delicate operation. I might have spilled some of it."

"Sorry." Wilson shook his head forlornly. "You appreciate the injustice of it all? I set up a scene expecting thanks, and end up apologizing. It happens every time."

"But I do thank you," Da Silva insisted. "I needed that drink."

Wilson studied his friend a moment and then reached for the bottle. "They're all gone?"

Da Silva nodded happily. "Every last little one. And about time. The final bunch left from Galeão about half an hour ago. After the head of their delegation made a touching speech about the hospitality of our fair country, and the beauty of our wonderful city." He shook his head envyingly. "It must be wonderful to be a policeman in some place where diplomats don't look for an excuse to visit. Some place like Kamchatka, for example."

"Or Pittsburgh," Wilson added, and grinned. "So now you can go back to taking your jacket off at lunch again."

"Right." Da Silva winked at him. "And about time for that, too. I was beginning to walk lopsided, and my maid complained that my jackets kept sliding off the hangers. My tailor also threatened suicide; he claimed I was frightening off custom." He leaned back, staring out of the large windows benevolently. "What a lovely day!"

"You sound relaxed," Wilson commented.

"Completely."

"Then, in that case," Wilson said slowly, "you might finally get around to clueing me in on that Dorcas case. You never did, you know. After you picked up brother Alvinor, you shut up like a clam. And this is the first time I've had a chance to talk to you since."

"That's right," Da Silva said slowly, and looked up thoughtfully. "I keep forgetting that you people didn't hire Sebastian, after all. Well, where do you want me to start?"

"How about at the beginning?"

"A reasonable request," Da Silva agreed equably, and then paused to put his thoughts in order. "Well, once

upon a time there were two brothers named Juan Dorcas and Alvinor Dorcas, who bore an extraordinary resem-
blance to each other, but who otherwise had little in
common. Alvinor was used to play and fun, while
brother Juan—"

Wilson raised a hand in interruption. "Let's not go
back to their nursery days. Let's take it from within the
last decade. For example, just how did you get onto
brother Alvinor?"

"Through you, of course. You got onto him for me,
and I thank you." Da Silva dipped his head in an exaggerated salute of appreciation. "When you were lucky
enough—" He studied the expression that had sprung to
Wilson's brow and modified his statement accordingly.
"I beg your pardon. I mean, when you were astute enough
to locate that ship with its first mate who was a camera-
bug, I happened to notice among that first batch of terrible pictures one photograph that oddly enough reminded me of Juan Dorcas. I'll admit it was just a faceless
figure leaning over the rail, but I'll also admit that at
the time I guess I had Juan Dorcas on the brain—"

"You didn't just have Juan Dorcas on the brain," Wilson commented sourly. "You also had the C.I.A. on the
brain. Or off the brain, rather."

Da Silva nodded brightly. "True." His heavy eyebrows
cocked quizzically. "Do you want to hear how I brilliantly
solved this case, or do you want to waste your time—plus
our entire lunch hour—angling for apologies?"

"Both," Wilson said firmly.

"Well, in that case we'll take my brilliance first. As I
was saying, I thought it rather strange that Dorcas would
travel on the same boat as a known killer—in fact, I
thought it strange he'd travel on a freighter at all. And I
thought it even more strange that I should get an anon-

ymous letter from Salvador de Bahia—where this ship docked about the time the letter was posted—advising us that Dorcas would be killed."

"Letter? What letter?" Wilson was frowning across the table. "You never told me anything about a letter."

Da Silva shrugged delicately. "I didn't want to hurt your feelings. The letter sort of hinted that your Government would be the ones most interested in the—ah, the removal—of Juan Dorcas, and knowing how inordinately touchy you had become on the subject . . ." He smiled and lifted his shoulders. "In any event, it suddenly occurred to me that possibly you might be telling the truth."

"Possibly!"

"Probably, then," Da Silva conceded. "When I was learning English, I was taught never to argue about an adverb. Anyway, I sent the letter and the photograph down to an old friend of mine in Montevideo and asked him to do some checking of handwriting in Buenos Aires, and he confirmed what had only been a wild hunch—"

"A hunch you had to fall back on because you hadn't been able to think of anything else."

"Exactly!" Da Silva made it sound as if he had just been complimented and appreciated it. "And I was right. The handwriting was that of brother Alvinor Dorcas. The picture, of course, was also of him, although I will freely admit it could have been of any short, faceless man. Even you." His hand went out for the bottle of cognac.

Wilson reached it first, poured himself a drink, and then proceeded to fill his companion's glass. "And Sebastian?"

"You brought us that," Da Silva said. "Among other things, his traveling to both Argentina and Portugal and then returning to Rio made it sound very much as if he was our boy. And also," he added honestly, "we didn't have the time to follow through on any other suspects. Not that we had any others. . . ."

Wilson frowned at his glass of cognac thoughtfully. "This Alvinor went to a lot of trouble, though. Hiring Sebastian so many months early, and taking the same boat just to see that Mendes actually got off in Rio. . . ."

"We don't know that that was his only reason. He preferred to be out of sight somewhere, and the boat was as good a place as any. And it also gave him a chance to post that letter in Salvador." He shrugged. "As to the trouble, it would have been worth it to him—or to anyone else in that position. After all, an assassination at the O.A.S. meeting would have been a perfect cover for a private killing, especially of a man as controversial as Juan Dorcas. So naturally he was forced to wait for the meeting to be held. And you want to remember he was playing for extremely high stakes. If it had worked, he would have been a very wealthy man."

Wilson nodded. "If he hadn't written that letter—"

"He wrote the letter as a clincher; as insurance. He didn't want me—or us, rather—led astray by anything as ridiculous as the truth." Da Silva shrugged. "I think even without it we'd have come up with the right answer in time. Especially the way you kept nagging me."

"Maybe," Wilson said. "And maybe not. If I hadn't been lucky enough—" He suddenly grinned. "Or, rather, astute enough—to be a trustee of Stranger's Hospital; or if Les Weldon hadn't been playing golf that morning and Dona Ilesia had gotten hold of him first with her story of the missing patient, then brother Alvinor might well have gotten away with it, because we'd never have gotten onto Mendes."

"He might still have had his troubles," Da Silva pointed out. "Because I would have still insisted on Juan Dorcas wearing that bullet-proof vest. Though I will admit having proof that a known assassin was gunning for him helped me to insist." He shook his head. "You'd think that after three previous attempts on his life he'd listen to reason, but I had to practically threaten him to get him to wear it." He suddenly grinned impishly. "I have a feeling he feels the way I do about clothes. A bullet-proof vest under a morning coat is bound to bunch up and wrinkle. And it must have been uncomfortable in the heat."

"Except that it saved his life."

"But only at the expense of a ruined shirtfront." Da Silva's smile disappeared; his eyes came up thoughtfully. "You know, when he was told it was his brother who tried to have him assassinated, he insisted on his government instituting extradition proceedings immediately, to transfer dear Alvinor out of our hands."

Wilson stared at him. "And you're going to let them have him? You're going to let him get away?"

Da Silva nodded slowly. "I think so. Of course it isn't in my department to say yes or no, but I'm definitely in favor."

"But why?"

"You see," Da Silva said slowly, "neither Brazil nor Argentina has a penalty for his crime that is either excessive or even equitable. The maximum here is thirty-three years, no matter how grave the crime, and nobody I know of has ever served more than half of this. But"—his dark eyes came up, expressionless—"I have a feeling that once Alvinor is in his big brother's backyard . . ."

Wilson nodded in sudden understanding. "Then you think his punishment may be more severe, is that it?"

"More certain, anyway," Da Silva said, and turned in his chair, searching for a waiter. He frowned. "Where the devil is everybody today?" He turned back. "Wilson, why don't you be a good fellow and go over to the maître d' and get us a waiter?"

Wilson stared at him. "You're marvelous! You manage to avoid an apology you still owe me, you completely overlook the fact that everything you had to help you in this case came from me and my efforts, you forget that once I was an associate, and then I was reduced to a suspect—and now I've come all the way down to being a servant." He shook his head. "What is this?"

Da Silva grinned at him. "Do you remember not so very long ago I asked you why the United States didn't send us more Wilsons, and you accused me of not knowing what to do with the Wilsons we had?"

"I do."

"Well, then," Da Silva said, spreading his hands in explanation, "I'm merely trying to find a use for the Wilsons we have. . . ."

The smaller man from the American Embassy stared across the table a moment, and then his face broke into a wide smile. "I knew if I waited long enough I'd get that apology," he said, and rose to his feet to get a waiter. . . .